THE CABIN
[LA BARRACA]

THE CABIN
[LA BARRACA]

BY

VICENTE BLASCO IBÁÑEZ

TRANSLATED FROM THE SPANISH BY
FRANCIS HAFFKINE SNOW
AND BEATRICE M. MEKOTA
WITH A NEW INTRODUCTION BY
JOHN GARRETT UNDERHILL

NEW YORK

Howard Fertig

1975

Library of Congress Cataloging in Publication Data
Blasco Ibáñez, Vicente, 1867-1928.
  The cabin = La barraca.
  Reprint of the ed. published by Knopf, New York.
  I. Title. II. Title: La barraca.
PZ3.B6125Cab14 [PQ6603.L2]   863'.6'2   75-1109

Printed in the United States of America

INTRODUCTION

Vicente Blasco Ibáñez was born in Valencia, that most typical of the cities of the western littoral of the Mediterranean, known as the Spanish Levant. Adventurous and buoyant, his career affords the strongest possible contrast to the traditional dignity and reserve which distinguish the Castilian of the interior plateau. The Valencian dialect is directly affiliated with the neighbouring Catalan and through it with the Provençal. In the character of the people there is a facility which suggests the French, while an Oriental element is distinctly evident, persisting not only from the days of the Moorish kingdoms, but eloquent of the shipping of the East and the *lingua franca* of the inland sea. Blasco Ibáñez is a Levantine touched with a suggestion of Cyprus, of Alexandria, with an adaptability and mobility of temperament which have endowed him with a faculty of literary improvisation which is extraordinary. He has been a novelist, a controversialist, a politician, a member of the Cortes, a republican, an orator, a traveller, an expatriate, a ranchman, a duellist, a journalist. "He writes," says the Argentine Manuel Ugarte, "as freely as other men talk. This is the secret of the freshness and charm of the unforgettable pages of *The Cabin,* of the sense of fraternity and *camara-*

1

derie which springs up immediately, uniting the author and his readers. He seems to be telling us a story between cigarettes at the café table. In these times when mankind is shaking itself free from stupid snobbery to return to nature and to simple sincerity, this gift of free and lucid expression is the highest of merits."

Ibáñez's first stories dealt with the life of the Valencian plain, whose marvellous fertility has become proverbial:

> Valencia is paradise;
> Wheat today, tomorrow rice.

Although favourably received, these early literary efforts appeared inconsequential beside his political triumphs, which speedily assured him prominence and resulted in the transfer of his activities to Madrid. From his birth, however, in 1867 until his election as a deputy to the Cortes, his thoughts centred upon his native province, and the works produced during this period beyond doubt constitute his major achievement. Swift with the dash and movement of the born storyteller and the vitality of a mind that is always at white heat, they are remarkable for vivid descriptive power through which each successive picture conveys an impression of the subject so intense that it seems plastic. Ibáñez never again rose to be so completely sincere. Here was a more robust Sorolla, a painter of sunshine, not as it idly fell on the slumberous streets of forgotten Andalusian cities, but turbulent with the surging of the spirit, welling up and pressing on. *The Cabin* and

Reeds and Mud were the principal glories of this Valencian, or regional, period and provide at once the foundation and crown of his reputation.

In the novel of a more intellectual, introspective nature he has also met with rare success, as William Dean Howells has pointed out in one of the few articles upon this author in English which are of value. The vein is more complex but not less copious, remaining instinct with power, yet it must be regarded in its genesis as alien to the national temper, an excursion into the processes of the northern mind. The documented realism of Zola betrays its presence in *The Cathedral* while a new psychologic element infuses the torrid emotionalism of *Blood and Sand* and *The Dead Command*. The true gifts of the analyst, nevertheless, were denied Ibáñez; neither was he an æsthete; in fact no phase of art could detain him long. He sailed for Argentina to deliver a series of lectures on patriotic themes at a time when Anatole France was upholding the Gallic tradition in that country. Argentine life attracted him and he became a ranchman on the Pampas, bought an American motor tractor, and settled down to create the Argentine novel. Though South America has produced excellent novelists it has as yet fostered none preeminently great, nor was Ibáñez to find its soil more propitious than had its native sons. His first attempt, *The Argonauts*, proved a failure. Again he changed continents, disappearing as suddenly as he came, and took up his residence in Paris, a city which had been to him from early youth a second home. This crisis co-

incided by a happy chance with the breaking out of the
World War and he entered the employ of the French
as a writer of propaganda for circulation among the
Spanish peoples, in the course of whose routine he
composed *The Four Horsemen of the Apocalypse*. The
fabulous success of this book in the English transla-
tion transformed him into a world figure overnight.
He was canonized, he was accepted abroad as the repre-
sentative Spaniard, the towering genius of his race.
Royalties poured in; the motion-picture extended its
hand; the United States welcomed him with a shower
of learned degrees, and he was enabled to pass the
sunset years of his life upon the Riviera as a formid-
able array of novels flowed from his pen whose profits
might well have awakened envy in the heart of the
elder Dumas. Writing in the cosmopolitan vortex of
the great war capital, he had interpreted the spirit of
the conflict in terms of the imagination with a force
and breadth of appeal such as were given in that day
to no other man. While Spain remained neutral under
compulsion of material conditions which those who understood her best appreciated at their true worth, in a
single volume Ibáñez contrived to abrogate the neutral-
ity of the land, and to marshal his people publicly
where their hearts had been privately, in line with the
progressive opinion of the world. The reaction upon
his personal fortunes, however, was not pleasant to
contemplate, except from a purely mercenary point of
view. None of the books which followed approached
literature. *Queen Calafia, The Enemies of Woman*—

the list is a commercial one, why recall names? A sequence of mysterious posthumous volumes brings the chapter to a close several years subsequent to his death, which took place in 1928.

If in *The Four Horsemen of the Apocalypse* Ibáñez proved most effective as a propagandist, in *The Cabin* he made his chief contribution to art. It is the most nicely rounded of his stories, the most perfect. Spanish and Latin-American opinion is here unanimous. Nevertheless, primarily it is a human document. Rubén Darío, than whom, certainly, none is better qualified to speak, emphasizes this crusading bias: "The soul of a gladiator, a robust teller of tales *à la* Zola, is externalized in *The Cabin*. The creative flood proceeds without faltering with a rapidity of invention which proclaims the riches of the source. Books such as this are not written purely for love of art, they embody profound human aspirations. They are beautiful pages not only, but generous deeds and apostolic exploits as well." The ambient blends admirably with the action and the characters to present a picture which is satisfying and which appeals to the eye as complete. *The Cabin* is a rarely visual story, and directly so, affording in this respect an interesting contrast to the imaginative suggestion of the present-day Castilian realists. In no other work has the author combined so effectively the broad swish of his valiant style with the homely, even crass detail which lends it significance. "A book like this," to quote Iglesias Hermida, "is written only once in a lifetime, and one book like this is sufficient."

A favourite anecdote of Blasco Ibáñez is so illuminative that it deserves to be told in his own words:

"When I go to the bull-ring, as I do from time to time with a foreigner, I enjoy the polychromatic animated spectacle of the crowded amphitheatre, the theatric entrance of the fighters and the encounters with the first bull. The second diverts me less, at the third I begin to yawn, and when the fourth appears, I reach for the book or newspaper which I have forehandedly brought along in my pocket. And I suspect that half of the spectators feel very much as I do.

"A number of years ago a professor in one of the celebrated universities of the United States came to visit me at Madrid, and I took him, as is customary, to see a bull-fight.

"This learned gentleman was also a man of action, a Roosevelt of the professorial chair; he rode, he boxed, he was devoted to hunting big game as well as to the exploration of unknown lands. He watched intently every incident of the fight, knitting his blond eyebrows above his spectacles—for he was near-sighted—as he did so. Occasionally he muttered a word of approbation: 'Very good!' 'Truly interesting!' I saw, however, that some new, original idea was crystallizing in his mind.

"When we came out, he expressed himself:

" 'Very interesting entertainment, but somewhat monotonous. Would it not be better to turn the six bulls loose simultaneously and then kill them all at once? It might shorten the exhibition, but how much more exciting! It would give those chaps an opportunity to show off their courage.'

"I looked upon that Yankee as upon a great sage. He had formulated definitely the vague dissatisfaction with the bull-fight which had lurked in my mind ever since, as a boy, I had suffered at the tiresome spectacle. Yes! Six bulls at one time!"

In the novel of Blasco Ibáñez, it is always six bulls at one time.

JOHN GARRETT UNDERHILL

THE CABIN
[LA BARRACA]

THE CABIN

I

THE vast plain stretched out under the blue splendour of dawn, a broad sash of light which appeared in the direction of the sea.

The last nightingales, tired of animating with their songs this autumn night, which seemed like spring in the balminess of its atmosphere, poured forth their final warble, as if the light of dawn wounded them with its steely reflections.

Flocks of sparrows arose like crowds of pursued urchins from the thatched roofs of the farmhouses, and the tops of the trees trembled at the first assault of these gamins of the air, who stirred up everything with the flurry of their feathers.

The sounds which fill the night had gradually died away: the babbling of the canals, the murmur of the cane-plantations, the bark of the watchful dog.

The *huerta* was awaking, and its yawnings
were growing ever noisier. The crowing of the
cock was carried on from farm-house to farm-
house; the bells of the village were answering,
with noisy peals, the ringing of the first mass
which floated from the towers of Valencia, blue
and hazy in the distance. From the corrals
came a discordant animal-concert; the whinny-
ing of horses, the lowing of gentle cows, the
clucking of hens, the bleating of lambs, the
grunting of pigs, . . . all the noisy awakening
of creatures who, upon feeling the first caress of
dawn, permeated with the pungent perfume of
vegetation, long to be off and run about the
fields.

Space became saturated with light; the shadows dissolved as though swallowed up by the
open furrows and the masses of foliage; and
in the hazy mist of dawn, humid and shining
rows of mulberry-trees, waving lines of cane-
brake, large square beds of garden vegetables
like enormous green handkerchiefs, and the
carefully tilled red earth, became gradually
more and more defined.

Along the high-road there came creeping rows
of moveable black dots, strung out like files of

ants, all marching toward the city. From all the ends of the *vega*, resounded the creaking of wheels mingled with idle songs interrupted by shouts urging on the beasts; and from time to time, like the sonorous heralding of dawn, the air was rent by the furious braying of the donkey protesting so to speak against the heavy labour which fell upon him with break of day.

Along the canals, the glassy sheet of ruddy crystal was disturbed by noisy plashings and loud beating of wings which silenced the frogs as the ducks advanced like galleys of ivory, moving their serpentine necks like fantastic prows.

The plain was flooded with light, and life penetrated into the interior of the farm-houses.

Doors creaked as they opened; under the grape-arbours white figures could be seen, which upon awakening stretched out, hands clasped behind their heads, and gazed toward the illumined horizon.

The stables stood with doors wide-open, vomiting forth a stream of milch-cows, herds of goats, and the nags of the cart-drivers, all bound for the city. From behind the screen of dwarfish trees which concealed the road, came the jingle of cow-bells, while mingling with their gay notes, there sounded the shrill *arre, aca!* [1] urging on the stubborn beasts.

At the doorways of the farm-houses stood those who were city-bound and those who remained to work in the fields, saluting each other.

May the Lord give us a good-day!

Good-day!

And after this salutation, exchanged with all the gravity of country folk who carry the blood of Moors in their veins, and who speak the name of God only with solemn gesture, silence fell again if the passer-by were one unknown; but if he were an intimate, he was commissioned with the purchase, in Valencia, of small objects for the house or wife.

The day had now completely dawned.

The air was already cleared of the tenuous mist that rose during the night from the damp fields and the noisy canals. The sun was coming out; in the ruddy furrows the larks hopped about with the joy of living one day more, and the mischievous sparrows, alighting at the still-closed windows, pecked away at the wood, chirp-

[1] Get up!

ing to those within, with the shrill cry of the
vagabond used to living at the expense of others:

"Up, you lazy drones! Work in the fields so
we may eat!"

Pepeta, wife of Toni, known throughout the
neighbourhood as Pimentó, had just entered their
barraca. She was a courageous creature, and
despite her pale flesh, wasted white by anaemia
while still in full youth, the most hard working
woman in the entire *huerta*. [1]

At daybreak, she was already returning from
market. She had risen at three, loaded herself with the baskets of garden-truck gathered
by Toni the night before, and groping for the
paths while she cursed the vile existence in which
she was worked so hard, had guided herself
like a true daughter of the *huerta* through the
darkness to Valencia. Meanwhile her husband,
that good fellow who was costing her so dearly,
continued to snore in the warm bed-chamber,
bundled in the matrimonial blankets.

The wholesalers who bought the vegetables
were well acquainted with this woman, who,

---

[1] A *huerta* is a cultivated district divided usually into tiny,
fertile, truck-garden and fruit farms.

even before the break of day, was already in the market-place of Valencia. Seated amid her baskets, she shivered beneath her thin, threadbare shawl while she gazed, with an envy of which she was not aware, at those who were drinking a cup of coffee to combat the morning chill the better. She hoped with a submissive, animal-like patience to get the money she had reckoned upon, in her complicated calculations, in order to maintain Toni and run the house.

When she had sold her vegetables, she returned home, running all the way, to save an hour on the road.

A second time she set forth to ply another trade; after the vegetables came the milk. And dragging the red cow by the halter, followed along by the playful calf which clung like an amorous satellite to its tail, Pepeta returned to the city, carrying a little stick under her arm, and a measuring-cup of tin with which to serve her customers.

La Rocha, as the cow was called on account of her reddish coat, mooed gently and trembled under her sackcloth cover as she felt the chill of morning, while she rolled her humid eyes toward the *barraca*, which remained behind with

its black stable and its heavy air, and thought
of the fragrant straw with the voluptuous desire
of sleep that is not satisfied.

Meanwhile, Pepeta urged her on with the
stick: it was growing late, and the customers
would complain. And the cow and little calf
trotted along the middle of the road of Alboraya,
which was muddy and furrowed with deep
ruts.

Along the sloping banks passed interminable
rows of cigarette-girls and silk-mill workers,
each with a hamper on one arm, while the other
swung free. The entire virginity of the *huerta*
went along this way toward the factories, leaving behind, with the flutter of their skirts, a
wake of harsh, rough chastity.

The blessing of God was over all the fields.

The sun rising like an enormous red wafer
from behind the trees and houses which hid the
horizon, shot forth blinding needles of gold.
The mountains in the background and the towers
of the city took on a rosy tint; the little clouds
which floated in the sky grew red like crimson
silk; the canals and the pools which bordered the
road seemed to become filled with fiery fish; the
swishing of the broom, the rattle of china, and

all the sounds of the morning's cleaning came from within the *barracas*.

The women squatted by the edges of the pools, with baskets of clothes for the wash at their sides; dark-grey rabbits came hopping along the paths with their deceiving smile, showing, in their flight, their reddish quarters, parted by the stub of a tail; with an eye red and flaming with anger, the cock mounted the heap of reddish manure with his peaceful odalisks about him and sent forth the cry of an irritated sultan.

Pepeta, oblivious to this awakening of dawn which she witnessed every day, hurried on her way, her stomach empty, her limbs aching, her poor clothing drenched with the perspiration characteristic of her pale, thin blood, which flowed for weeks at a time contrary to the laws of Nature.

The crowds of labouring people who were entering Valencia filled all the bridges. Pepeta passed the labourers from the surburbs who had come with their little breakfast-sacks over their shoulders, and stopped at the *octroi* to get her receipt,—a few coins which grieved her soul anew each day,—then went on through the deserted streets, whose silence was broken by the cowbells of *La Rocha*, a monotonous pastoral melody, which caused the drowsy townsman to dream of green pastures and idyllic scenery.

Pepeta had customers in all parts of the city. She went her intricate way through the streets, stopping before the closed doors; it was a blow on a knocker here, three or more repeated raps there, and ever the continuation of the strident, high-pitched cry, which it seemed could not possibly come from a chest so poor and flat:

La lleeet!

And the dishevelled, sunken-eyed servant came down in slippers, jug in hand, to receive the milk; or the aged concierge appeared, still wearing the mantilla which she had put on to go to mass.

By eight all the customers had been served. Pepeta was now near the Fishermen's quarter.

Here she had business also, and the poor farmer's wife bravely penetrated the dirty alleys which, at this hour, seemed to be dead. She always felt at first a certain uneasiness,—the instinctive repugnance of a delicate stomach: but her spirit, that of a woman who, though ill, was respectable, succeeded in rising above it, and she went on with a certain proud satisfaction.—

the pride of a chaste woman who consoles herself
by remembering that though bent and weakened
by her poverty, she is still superior to others.

From the closed and silent houses came forth
the breath of the cheap, noisy, shameless rabble mingled with an odour of heated, rotting
flesh; and through the cracks of the doors, there
seemed to escape the gasping and brutal breathing of heavy sleep, after a night of wild-beast caresses and amorous, drunken desires.

Pepeta heard some one calling her. At the
entrance to a narrow stairway stood a sturdy
girl, making signs to her. She was ugly, without any other charm than that of youth disappearing already; her eyes were humid, her
hair twisted in a topknot, and her cheeks, still
stained by the rouge of the preceding night,
seemed like a caricature of the red daubs on the
face of a clown,—a clown of vice.

The peasant woman, tightening her lips with
a grimace of pride and disdain, in order that the
distance between them might be well-marked,
began to fill a jar which the girl gave her with
milk from La Rocha's udders. The latter, however, did not take her eyes from the farmer's
wife.

"Pepeta,"—she said, in an indecisive voice, as though she were uncertain if it were really she.

Pepeta raised her head; she fixed her eyes for the first time upon the girl; then she also appeared to be in doubt.

"Rosario,—is it you?"

Yes, it was; with sad nods of the head she confirmed it. Pepeta immediately showed her surprise. She here! A daughter of such honourable parents! God! What shame!

The prostitute, through professional habit, tried to receive those exclamations of the scandalized farmer's wife with a cynical smile and the sceptical expression of one who has been initiated into the secret of life, and who believes in nothing; but Pepeta's clear eyes seemed to shame the girl, and she dropped her head as though she were about to weep.

No: she was not bad. She had worked in the factories, she had been a servant, but finally, her sisters, tired of suffering hunger, had given her the example. So here she was, sometimes receiving caresses, and sometimes receiving blows, and here she would stay till she ceased to live forever. It was natural: any family may

end thus where there is no mother nor father left.
The cause of it all was the master of the land;
he was to blame for everything, that Don Salvador, who assuredly must be burning in hell!
Ah, thief! How he had ruined the entire family!

Pepeta forgot her frigid attitude and cold reserve in order to join in the girl's indignation.
It was the truth, the whole truth! That avaricious old miser was to blame.   The entire *huerta*
knew it! Heaven save us! How easily a family may be ruined! And poor old Barret had
been so good! If he could only raise his head
and see his daughters! . . . It was well-known
yonder that the poor father had died in Ceuta
two years before; and as for the mother, the poor
widow had ended her suffering on a hospital-
bed.

What changes take place in the world in ten
years! Who would have said to her, and her sisters, who were reigning like queens in their
homes at the time, that they would come to such
an end? Oh Lord! Lord! Deliver us from
evil!

Rosario became animated during this conversation; she seemed rejuvenated by this friend of

her childhood. Her eyes, previously dead, sparkled as she recalled the past.

And the *barraca?* And the land? They were still deserted. Truly? That pleased her;—let them go to smash,—let them go to rack and ruin,—those sons of the rascally don Salvador.

That alone seemed to console her: she was very grateful to Pimentó and to all the others, because they had prevented those people yonder from coming to work the land which rightfully belonged to the family. And if any one wished to take possession of it, he knew only too well the remedy. . . . Bang! A report from a gun which would blow his head off!

The girl grew bolder; her eyes gleamed fiercely; within the passive breast of the prostitute, accustomed to blows, there came to life the daughter of the *huerta,* who, from very birth, has seen the musket hung behind the door, and breathed in the smell of gunpowder on feast-days with delight.

After speaking of the sad past Rosario, whose curiosity was awakened, went on inquiring about all the folks at home, and ended by noticing how badly Pepeta looked. Poor thing! It was per-

fectly apparent that she was not happy. Although still young, her eyes, clear, guileless, and
timid as a virgin's, alone revealed her real age.
Her body was a mere skeleton, and her reddish
hair, the colour of a tender ear of corn, was
streaked with grey though as yet she had not
reached her thirtieth year.

What kind of a life was Pimentó giving her?
Always drunk and averse to work? She had
brought it upon herself, marrying him contrary
to every one's advice. He was a strapping fellow, that was true; every one feared him in the
tavern of Copa on Sunday evenings, when he
played cards with the worst bullies of the
huerta; but in the house, he was bound to prove
an insufferable husband. Still, after all, men
are all alike! Perhaps she didn't know it!
Dogs, all of them, not worth the trouble of being
looked after! Great Heavens! how ill poor Pepeta was looking!

The loud, deep voice of a virago resounded
like a clap of thunder down the narrow stairway.

"Elisa! Bring up the milk at once! The
gentleman is waiting!"

Rosario began to laugh as though mad. "I
am called Elisa now! You didn't know that!"

It was a requirement of her business to change
her name, as well as to speak with an Andalusian
accent.   And she began to imitate the voice of
the virago upstairs with a species of rough hu-
mour.

But in spite of her mirth, she was in a hurry
to get away.   She was afraid of those upstairs.
The owner of the rough voice or the gentleman
who wanted the milk might give her some me-
mento of the delay.   So she hurried up after
urging Pepeta to stop again some other time to
tell her the news of the *huerta.*

The monotonous tinkling of the bell of
La Rocha continued for more than an hour
through the streets of Valencia; the wilted udders yielded up their last drop of insipid milk,
produced by a miserable diet of cabbage-leaves
and garbage, and Pepeta finally was ready to
start back toward the *barraca.*

The poor labouring-woman walked along
sadly deep in thought.   The encounter had impressed her; she remembered, as though it had
just happened the day before, the terrible tragedy
which had swallowed up old Barret and his entire family.

Since then, the fields, which his ancestors had

tilled for more than a hundred years, had lain abandoned at the edge of the high road.

The uninhabited *barraca* was slowly crumbling to pieces without any merciful hand to mend the roof or to cast a handful of clay upon the chinks in the wall.

Ten years of passing and re-passing had accustomed people to the sight of this ruin, so they paid no further attention to it. It had been some time since even Pepeta had looked at it. It now interested only the boys who, inheriting the hatred of their fathers, trampled down the nettles of the abandoned fields in order to riddle the deserted house with rocks, which split great gaps in the closed door, or to fill up the well under the ancient grape-arbour with earth and stones.

But this morning Pepeta, under the spell of the recent meeting, not only looked at the ruin, but stopped at the edge of the highway to see it the better.

The fields of old Barret, or rather, of the Jew, Don Salvador, and his excommunicated heirs, were an oasis of misery and abandonment in the midst of the *huerta,* so fertile, well-tilled, and smiling.

Ten years of desolation had hardened the soil, causing all the parasitic plants, all the nettles which the Lord has created to chasten the farmer, to spring up out of its sterile depths. A dwarfish forest, tangled and deformed, spread itself out over those fields in waving ranks of strange green tones, varied here and there by flowers, mysterious and rare, of the sort which thrive only amid cemeteries and ruins.

Here, in the rank maze of this thicket, fostered by the security of their retreat, there bred and multiplied all species of loathsome vermin, which spread out into the neighbouring fields; green lizards with corrugated loins, enormous beetles with shells of metallic reflection, spiders with short and hairy legs, and even snakes, which slid off to the adjoining canals. Here they thrived in the midst of the beautiful and cultivated plain, forming a separate estate, and devouring one another. Though they caused some damage to the farmers, the latter respected them even with a certain veneration, for the seven plagues of Egypt would have seemed but a trifle to the dwellers of the *huerta* had they descended upon those accursed fields.

The lands of old Barret never had been destined for man, so let the most loathsome pests nest among them, and the more, the better.

In the midst of these fields of desolation, which stood out in the beautiful plain like a soiled patch on a royal robe of green velvet, the *barraca* rose up, or one should rather say fell away, its straw roof bursting open, showing through the gaps, which the rain and wind had pierced, the worm-eaten framework of wood within.

The walls, rotted away by the rains, laid bare the clay-adobe. Only some very light stains revealed the former whitewash; the door was ragged along the lower edge which rats had gnawed, with wide cracks that ran, full length, from end to end. The two or three little windows, gaping wide, hung loosely on one hinge exposed to the mercy of the south-west winds, ready to fall as soon as the first gust should shake them.

This ruin hurt the spirit and weighed upon the heart. It seemed as though phantoms might sally forth from the wretched and abandoned hut as soon as darkness closed in; that from the interior might come the cries of the assassinated, rending the night; that all this waste of weeds might be a shroud to conceal hundreds of tragic corpses from sight.

Horrible were the visions which were conjured up by the contemplation of these desolate fields; and their gloomy poverty was sharpened by the contrast with the surrounding fields, so red and well-cultivated, with their orderly rows of garden-truck and their little fruit-trees, to whose leaves the autumn gave a yellowish transparency.

Even the birds fled from these plains of death, perhaps from fear of the hideous reptiles which stirred about under the growth of weeds, or possibly because they scented the vapour of abandonment.

If anything were seen to flutter over the broken roof of straw, it was certain to be of funereal plumage with black and treacherous wings, which as they stirred, cast silence over the joyful flappings and playful twitterings in the trees, leav- the *huerta* deathly still, as though no sparrows chirped within a half-league roundabout.

Pepeta was about to continue on her way toward her farmhouse, which peered whitely among the trees some distance across the fields; but she had to stand still at the steep edge of the highroad in order to permit the passing of a

loaded wagon, which seemed to be coming from
the city, and which advanced with violent
lurches.

At the sight of it, her feminine curiosity was
aroused.

It was the poor cart of a farmer drawn by an
old and bony nag, which was being helped over
the deep ruts by a tall man, who marched along-
side the horse, encouraging him with shouts and
the cracking of a whip.

He was dressed like a labourer; but his manner of wearing the handkerchief knotted around
the head, his corduroy trousers, and other details
of his costume, indicated that he was not from
the *huerta*, where personal adornment had gradually been corrupted by the fashions of the city.
He was a farmer from some distant *pueblo*; he
had come, perhaps, from the very centre of the
province.

Heaped high upon the cart, forming a pyra-
mid which mounted higher even than the side-
poles, was piled a jumble of domestic objects.
This was the migration of an entire family.
Thin mattresses, straw-beds, filled with rustling
leaves of corn, rush-seats, frying-pans, kettles,
plates, baskets, green bed-slats: all were heaped

upon the wagon, dirty, worn, and miserable, speaking of hunger, of desperate flight, as if disgrace stalked behind the family, treading at its heels. And on top of this disordered mass were three children, embracing each other as they looked out across the fields with wide-open eyes, like explorers visiting a country for the first time.

Treading close at the heels of the wagon, watching vigilantly to see that nothing might fall, trudged a woman with a slender girl, who appeared to be her daughter. At the other side of the nag, aiding him whenever the cart stuck in a rut, stalked a boy of some eleven years. His grave exterior was that of a child accustomed to struggle with misery. He was already a man at an age when others were still playing. A little dog, dirty and panting, brought up the rear.

Pepeta, leaning on the flank of her cow, and possessed with growing curiosity, watched them pass on. Where could these poor people be going?

This road, running into the fork of Alboraya, did not lead anywhere; it was lost in the distance as though exhausted by the innumerable fork-

ings of its lanes and paths, which gave entrance
to the various *barracas*.

But her curiosity had an unexpected gratifica-
tion. Holy Virgin! The wagon turned away
from the road, crossed the tumbledown little
bridge made of tree-trunks and sod which gave
access to the accursed fields, and went on through
the meadows of old Barret, crushing the hitherto
respected growth of weeds beneath its wheels.

The family followed behind, manifesting by
gestures and confused words, the impression
which this miserable poverty and decay were
making upon them, but all the while going directly in a straight line toward the ruined *barraca*
like those who are taking possession of their
own.

Pepeta did not stop to see more; she fairly
flew toward her own home. In order to arrive
the sooner, she abandoned the cow and little
calf, who tranquilly pursued their way like animals who have a good, safe stable and are not
worried about the course of human affairs.

Pimentó was lazily smoking, as he lay
stretched out at the side of his *barraca* with his
gaze fixed upon three little sticks smeared with
bird-lime, which shone in the sun, and about

which some birds were fluttering,—the occupation of a gentleman.

When he saw his wife arrive with astonished eyes and her weak chest panting, Pimentó changed his position in order to listen the better, at the same time warning her not to come near the little sticks.

What was up now? Had the cow been stolen from her?

Pepeta, between weariness and emotion, was scarcely able to utter two consecutive words.

The lands of Barret, . . . an entire family, . . . were going to work; they were going to live in the ruined *barraca,*—she had seen it herself!

Pimentó, a hunter with bird-lime, an enemy of labour, and the terror of the entire community, was no longer able to preserve his composure, the impressive gravity of a great lord, before such unexpected news.

Cordons!

And with one bound, he raised his heavy, muscular frame from the ground, and set out on a run without awaiting further explanations.

His wife watched him as he hurried across the fields until he reached a cane-brake adjoin-

ing the accursed land. Here he knelt down,
threw himself face forward, crawling upon his
belly as he spied through the cane-brake like a
Bedouin in ambush. After a few minutes, he
began to run again, and was soon lost to sight
amid the labyrinth of paths, each of which led
off to a different *barraca*, to a field where bending figures wielded large steel hoes, which glit-
tered as the light struck upon them.

The *huerta* lay smiling and rustling, filled
with whisperings and with light, drowsy under
the cascade of gold reflected from the morning
sun.

But soon there came, from the distance, the
mingled sound of cries and halloes. The news
passed on from field to field. With loud shouts,
with a trembling of alarm, of surprise, of indignation, it ran on through all the plain as though
centuries had not elapsed, and the report were
being spread that an Algerian galley was about
to land upon the beach, seeking a cargo of
white flesh.

II

AT harvest time, when old Barret gazed at the various plots into which his fields were divided, he was unable to restrain a feeling of pride. As he gazed upon the tall wheat, the cabbage-heads with their hearts of fleecy lace, the melons showing their green backs on a level with the earth, the pimentoes and tomatoes, half-hidden by their foliage, he praised the goodness of the earth as well as the efforts of all his ancestors for working these fields better than the rest of the *huerta*.

All the blood of his forefathers was here. Five or six generations of Barrets had passed their lives working this same soil. They had turned it over and over, taking care that its vital nourishment should not decrease, combing and caressing it with ploughshare and hoe; there was not one of these fields which had not been watered by the sweat and blood of the family.

The farmer loved his wife dearly, and even

forgave her the folly of having given him four daughters and no son, to help him in his work. Not that he loved his daughters any the less, angels sent from God who passed the day singing and sewing at the door of their farm-house, and who sometimes went out into the fields in order to give their poor father a little rest. But the supreme passion of old Barret, the love of all his loves, was the land upon which the silent and monotonous history of his family had unrolled.

Many years ago, many indeed, in those days when old Tomba, an aged man now nearly blind, who took care of the poor herd of a butcher at Alboraya, went roaming about in the band of The Friar, [1] shooting at the French, these lands had belonged to the monks of San Miguel de los Reyes.

They were good, stout gentlemen, sleek and voluble, who were not in a hurry to collect their rentals, and appeared to be satisfied if when they passed the cabin of an evening, the grand-

[1] Translator's Note:—Asensis Nebot, a Franciscan monk, surnamed El Fraile (The Friar), leader of a band of foot soldiers and cavalry in the War of Independence (1810–12) : he waged a guerilla warfare against the French around Valencia until the city was taken.

mother, who was a generous soul, would treat
them to deep cups of chocolate, and the first
fruits of the season. Before, long before, the
owner of all this land had been a great lord, who
upon dying, had unloaded both his sins and his
estates upon the bosom of the community. Now,
alas! they belonged to Don Salvador, a little,
dried-up old man of Valencia, who so tormented
old Barret, that he even dreamed of him at
night.

The poor farmer kept his trouble hidden from
his family. He was a courageous man of clean
habits. If he went to the tavern of Copa for a
while on Sundays, when all the people of the
neighbourhood were gathered there together, it
was in order to watch the card-players, to laugh
heartily at the absurdities and brutalities of Pimentó, and the other strapping young fellows who
played "cock o' the walk" about the *huerta;* but
never did he approach a counter to buy a glass;
he always kept his sash-purse tight around the
waist, and if he drank at all, it was only when
one of the winners was treating all the crowd.

Averse to discussing his difficulties, he always seemed to be smiling, good-natured and
calm, with the blue cap which had won for him

his nickname,[1] pulled well down over his ears.

He worked from daylight until dusk. While the rest of the *huerta* still slept, he tilled his fields in the uncertain light of dawn, but more and more convinced, all the time, that he could not go on working them alone.

It was too great a burden for one man. If he only had a son! When he sought aid, he took on servants who robbed him, worked but little, and whom he discharged when he surprised them asleep in the stable during the sunny hours.

Obsessed with his respect for his ancestors, he would rather have died in his fields, overcome by fatigue, than rent a single acre to strange hands. And since he could not manage all the work alone, half of his fertile land remained fallow and unproductive, while he tried to maintain his family and pay off his landlord by the cultivation of the other half.

A silent struggle was this, desperate and obstinate, to earn enough for the necessities of life and overcome the ebbing of his vitality.

He now had only one wish. It was that his little girls should not know; that no one should

[1] Barrete means "a round hat without a visor." Translator's note.

give them an inkling of the worries and troubles which harassed their father; that the sacred joy of this household, the joy enlivened at all hours by the songs and laughter of the four sisters, who had been born in four successive years, should not be broken.

And they, in the meantime, had already begun to attract the attention of the young swains of the *huerta*, when they went to the merrymakings of the village in their new and showy silk hand-kerchiefs and their rustling ironed skirts. And while they were getting up at dawn and slipping off barefooted in their chemises in order to look down, through the cracks of the little windows, at the suitors who were singing the *albaes*, [1] or who wooed them with thrummings of the guitar, poor old Barret, trying harder and harder to bal-ance his accounts, drew out ounce by ounce the handful of gold which his father had amassed for him farthing by farthing, and tried in vain to appease Don Salvador, the old miser who never had enough, and who, not content with squeezing him, kept talking of the bad times, the scandalous increase in taxes, and the need of raising his rent.

Barret could not possibly have had a worse

[1] "Dawn-Songs," serenades at dawn. Translator's note.

landlord. He bore a detestable reputation
throughout the entire *huerta,* since there was
hardly a district where he did not own property.
Every evening he passed over the roads, visiting
his tenants, wrapped up even in springtime in
his old cloak, shabby and looking like a beggar,
while maledictions and hostile gestures followed
after him. It was the tenacity of avarice which
desired to be in contact with its property at all
hours; the persistency of the usurer, who has
pending accounts to settle.

The dogs howled from a distance when they
saw him, as though Death itself were approaching; the children looked after him with frowning
faces; men hid themselves in order to avoid painful excuses, and the women came to meet him at
the door of the cabin with their eyes upon the
ground and the lie ready to entreat him to be
patient, while they answered his blustering
threats with tears.

Pimentó who, as the public bully, interested
himself in the misfortunes of his neighbours, and
who was the knight-errant of the *huerta,* muttered something through his teeth which sounded
like the promise of a thrashing, with a cooling-off
later in a canal. But the very victims of the

miser held him back, telling him of the influence of Don Salvador, warning him that he was a man who spent his mornings in court and had powerful friends. With such, the poor are always losers.

Of all his tenants, the best was Barret, who at the cost of great effort owed him nothing at all. And the old miser, even while pointing him out as a model to the other tenants, carried his cruelty toward him to the utmost extreme. Aroused by the very meekness of the farmer he showed himself more exacting, and was evidently pleased to find a man upon whom he could vent without fear all his instincts of robbery and oppression.

Finally he raised the rent of the land. Barret protested, even wept as he recited to him the merits of the family who had worked the skin from their hands in order to make these fields the best of the *huerta*. But Don Salvador was inflexible. Were they the best? Then he ought to pay more. And Barret paid the increase; he would give up his last drop of blood before he would abandon those fields which little by little were taking his very life.

At last he had no money left to tide him over. He could count only upon the produce from the

fields. And completely alone, poor Barret concealed the real situation from his family. He
forced himself to smile when his wife and daughters begged him not to work so hard, and he kept
on like a veritable madman.

He did not sleep; it seemed to him that his garden-truck was growing less quickly than that
of his neighbours; he made up his mind that
he, and he alone, should cultivate all the land;
he worked at night, groping in the darkness; the
slightest threatening cloud would make him
tremble, and be fairly beside himself with fear;
and finally, honourable and good as he was, he
even took advantage of the carelessness of his
neighbours and robbed them of their share of
water for the irrigation.

But if his family were blind, the neighbouring
farmers understood his situation and pitied him
for his meekness. He was a big, good-natured
fellow, who did not know how to put on a bold
front before the repellent miser, who was slowly
draining him dry.

And this was true. The poor fellow, exhausted by his feverish existence and mad labour, became a mere skeleton of skin and bones,
bent over like an octogenarian, with sunken eyes.

That characteristic cap, which had given him his nickname, no longer remained settled upon his ears, but as he grew leaner, drooped toward his shoulders, like the funereal extinguisher of his existence.

But the worst of it was that this insufferable excess of fatigue only served to pay half of what the insatiable monster demanded. The consequences of his mad labours were not slow in coming. Barret's nag, a long-suffering animal, the companion of all his frantic toil, tired of working both day and night, of drawing the cart with loads of garden-truck to the market at Valencia, and of being hitched to the plough without time to breathe or to cool off, decided to die rather than to attempt the slightest rebellion against his poor master.

Then indeed the poor farmer saw himself lost! He gazed with desperation at his fields which he could no longer cultivate; the rows of fresh garden-truck which the people in the city devoured indifferently without suspecting the anxiety the produce had caused the poor farmer, in the constant battle with his poverty and with the land.

But Providence, which never abandons the

poor, spoke to him through the mouth of Don
Salvador. Not vainly do they say that God
often derives good from evil.

The insufferable miser, the voracious usurer,
offered his assistance with touching and paternal
kindness on hearing of Barret's misfortune.
How much did he need to buy another beast?
Fifty dollars? Then here he was, ready to aid
him, and to show him how unjust was the hatred
of those who despised and spoke ill of him.

And he loaned money to Barret, although with
the insignificant detail of demanding that he
place his signature (since business is business),
at the foot of a certain paper in which he men-
tioned interest, the accumulation of interest, and
security for the debt, listing to cover this last
detail, the furniture, the implements, all that the
farmer possessed on his farm, including the animals of the corral.

Barret, encouraged by the possession of a new
and vigorous young horse, returned to his work
with more spirit, to kill himself again over those
lands which were crushing him, and which
seemed to grow in proportion as his efforts diminished until they enveloped him like a red
shroud.

All that his fields produced was eaten by his family, and the handful of copper which he made by his sales in the market of Valencia was soon scattered; he could never eke out enough to satisfy the avarice of Done Salvador.

The anguish of old Barret over his struggle to pay his debt and his failure to do so aroused in him a certain instinct of rebellion which caused all sorts of confused ideas of justice to surge through his crude reasoning. Why were not the fields his own? All his ancestors had spent their lives upon these lands; they were sprinkled with the sweat of his family; if it were not for them, the Barrets, these lands would be as depopulated as the sands of the seashore. And now this inhuman old man, who was the master here, though he did not know how to pick up a hoe and had never bent his back in toil in his whole life, was putting the screws on him and crushing him with all his "reminders." Christ! How the affairs of men are ordered!

But these revolts were only momentary; the resigned submission of the labourer returned to him; with his traditional and superstitious respect for property. He must work and be honest.

And the poor man, who considered that failure to pay one's obligation was the greatest of all dishonours, returned to his work, growing ever weaker and thinner, and feeling within himself the gradual sagging of his vitality. Convinced that he would not be able to drag out the situation much longer, he was yet indignant at the mere possibility of abandoning a handful of the lands of his forefathers.

When Christmas came, he was able to pay Don Salvador only a small part of the half-year's rent that fell due; Saint John's day arrived, and he had not a *centime;* his wife was sick; he had even sold their wedding jewelry in order to meet expenses; . . . the ancient pendant earrings, and the collar of pearls, which were the family treasure, and the future possession of which had given rise to discussions among the four daughters.

The avaricious old miser proved himself to be inflexible. No, Barret, this could not continue. Since he was kind-hearted (however unwilling people were to believe it), he would not permit the farmer to kill himself in his determination to cultivate more land than his efforts were equal to. No, he would not consent to it; he was too kind-hearted. And as he had re-

ceived another offer of rental, he notified Barret
to relinquish the fields as soon as possible. He
was very sorry, but he also was poor. Ah!
And at the same time, he reminded him that it
would be necessary to pay back the loan for
the purchase of the horse, . . . a sum which
with the interest amounted to . . .

The poor farmer did not even pay attention to
the sum of some thousand reals to which his
debt had aggregated with the blessed interest,
so agitated and confused did he become by this
order to abandon his lands.

His weakness and the inner erosion produced
by the crushing struggle of two years showed
themselves suddenly.

He, who had never wept, now sobbed like a
child. All of his pride, his Moorish gravity,
disappeared all at once, and kneeling down before the old man, he begged him not to forsake
him since he looked upon him as a father.

But a fine father poor Barret had picked!
Don Salvador proved to be relentless. He was
sorry, but he could not help it: he himself was
poor; he had to provide a living for his sons.
And he continued to cloak his cruelty with sentences of hypocritical sentimentality.

The farmer grew tired of asking for mercy. He made several trips to Valencia to the house of the master to remind him of his forefathers, of his moral right to those lands, begging him for a little patience, declaring with frenzied hope that he would pay him back. But at last the miser refused to open his door to him.

Then desperation gave Barret new life. He became again the son of the *huerta*, proud, spirited, intractable, when he is convinced that he is in the right. The landlord did not wish to listen to him? He refused to give him any hope? Very well; he was in his own house; if Don Salvador desired anything, he would have to seek him there. He would like to see the bully who could make him leave his farm.

And he went on working, but with misgiving, gazing anxiously about if any one unknown to him happened to be approaching over the adjoining roads, as though expecting at any moment to be attacked by a band of bandits.

They summoned him to court, but he did not appear.

He already knew what this meant: the snares that men set in order to ruin the honourable. If they were going to rob him, let them seek

him out on these lands which had become a part
of his very flesh and blood, for as such he would
defend them.

One day they gave him notice that the court
was going to begin proceedings to expel him from
his land that very afternoon; furthermore, they
would attach everything he had in his cabin to
meet his debts.   He would not be sleeping there
that night.

This news was so incredible to poor old Barret that he smiled with incredulity.   This might
happen to others, to those cheats who had never
paid anything; but he, who had always fulfilled
his duty, who had even been born here, who
owed only a year's rent,—nonsense!   Such a
thing could not happen, even though one were
living among savages, without charity or re-
ligion!

But in the afternoon, when he saw certain men
in black coming along the road, big funereal
birds with wings of paper rolled under the arm,
he no longer was in doubt.   This was the enemy.
They were coming to rob him.

And suddenly there was awakened within old
Barret the blind courage of the Moor who will
suffer every manner of insult but who goes

mad when his property is touched.   Running
into the cabin, he seized the old shot-gun, always hung loaded behind the door, and raising it
to his shoulder, took his stand under the vineyard, ready to put two bullets into the first bandit
of the law to set foot upon his fields.

His sick wife and four daughters came running
out, shouting wildly, and threw themselves upon
him, trying to wrest away the gun, pulling at the
barrel with both hands.   And such were the
cries of the group, as they struggled and con-
tended for it, reeling from one pillar of the
grape-arbour to the other, that people from the
neighbourhood began to run out, arriving in an
anxious crowd, with the fraternal solidarity of
those who live in deserted places.

It was Pimentó who prudently made himself
master of the shot-gun and carried it off to his
house.   Barret staggered behind, trying to pur-
sue him but restrained and held fast by the strong
arms of some strapping young fellows, while he
vented his madness upon the fool who was keeping him from defending his own.

"Pimentó,—thief!   Give me back my shot-
gun!"

But the bully smiled good-naturedly, satisfied
that he was behaving both prudently and pater-
nally with the old madman. Thus he brought
him to his own farm-house, where he and Barret's friends watched him and advised him not
to do a foolish deed. Have a care, old Barret!
These people are from the court, and the poor
always lose when they pick a quarrel with *it!*
Coolness and evil design succeed above everything.

And at the same time, the big black birds were
writing papers, and yet more papers in the farm-
house of Barret; impassively they turned over
the furniture and the clothing, making an inven-
tory even of the corral and the stable, while the
wife and the daughters wept in despair, and the
terrified crowd, gathering at the door, followed
all the details of the deed, trying to console the
poor woman, or breaking out into suppressed
maledictions against the Jew, Don Salvador, and
these fellows who yielded obedience to such a
dog.

Toward nightfall, Barret, who was like one
overwhelmed, and who, after the mad crisis, had
fallen into a stony stupor, saw some bundles of

clothing at his feet, and heard the metallic sound of a bag which contained his farming implements.

"Father! Father!" whimpered the tremulous voices of his daughters, who threw themselves into his arms; behind them the old woman, sick, trembling with fever, and in the rear, invading the *barraca* of Pimentó, and disappearing into the background through the dark door, all the people of the neighbourhood, the terrified chorus of the tragedy.

He had already been driven away from his farmhouse. The men in black had closed it, taking away the keys; nothing remained to them there except the bundles which were on the floor; the worn clothing, the iron implements; this was all which they were permitted to take out of the house.

Their words were broken by sobs; the father and the daughters embraced again, and Pepeta, the mistress of the house, as well as other women, wept and repeated the maledictions against the old miser until Pimentó opportunely intervened.

There would be time left to speak of what had occurred; now it was time for supper. What the deuce! Grieve like this because of an old Jew!

If he could but see all this, how his evil heart would rejoice! The people of the *huerta* were kind; all of them would help to care for the family of old Barret, and would share with them a loaf of bread if they had nothing more.

The wife and daughters of the ruined farmer went off with some neighbours to pass the night in their houses. Old Barret remained behind, under the vigilance of Pimentó.

The two men remained seated until ten in their rush-chairs, smoking cigar after cigar in the candle-light.

The poor old farmer appeared to be crazy. He answered in short monosyllables the reflections of this bully, who now assumed the rôle of a good-natured fellow; and when he spoke it was always to repeat the same words:

"Pimentó! Give me my shot-gun!"

And Pimentó smiled with a sort of admiration. The sudden ferocity of this little old man, who was considered a good-natured fool by all the *huerta*, astounded him. Return him the shot-gun! At once! He well divined by the straight wrinkles which stood out between his eyebrows, his firm intention of blowing the author of his ruin to atoms.

Barret grew more and more vexed with the young fellow. He went so far as to call him a thief: he had refused to give him his weapon. He had no friends; he could see that well enough; all of them were only ingrates, equal to don Salvador in avarice; he did not wish to sleep here; he was suffocating. And searching in the bag of implements, he selected a sickle, shoved it through his sash, and left the farmhouse. Nor did Pimentó attempt to bar his way.

At such an hour, he could do no harm; let him sleep in the open if it suited his pleasure. And the bully, closing the door, went to bed.

Old Barret started directly toward the fields, and like an abandoned dog, began to make a détour around his farmhouse.

Closed! Closed forever! These walls had been raised by his grandfather and renovated by himself through all these years. Even in the darkness, the pallor of the neat whitewash, with which his little girls had coated them three months before, stood out plainly.

The corral, the stable, the pigsties were all the work of his father; and this straw-roof, so slender and high, with the two little crosses at the ends, he had built himself as a substitution for the old, which had leaked everywhere.

And the curbstone at the well, the post of the vineyard, the cane-fences over which the pinks and the morning-glories were showing their tufts of bloom;—these too were the work of his hands. And all this was going to become the property of another, because—yes, because men had arranged it so.

He searched in his sash for the pasteboard strip of matches in order to set fire to the straw-roof. Let the devil fly away with it all; it was his own, anyway, as God knew, and he could destroy his own property and would do so before he would see it fall into the hands of thieves.

But just as he was going to set fire to his old house, he felt a sensation of horror, as if he saw the ghosts of all his ancestors rising up before him; and he hurled the strip of matches to the ground.

But the longing for destruction continued roaring through his head, and sickle in hand, he set forth over the fields which had been his ruin.

Now at a single stroke he would get even with the ungrateful earth, the cause of all his misfortunes.

The destruction lasted for entire hours.
Down they came tumbling to his heels, the arches
of cane upon which the green tendrils of the
tender kidney-beans and peas were climbing;
parted by the furious sickle, the beans fell, and
the cabbages and lettuce, driven by the sharp
steel, flew wide like severed heads, scattering
their rosettes of leaves all around. No one
should take advantage of his labour.

And thus he went on mowing until the break of
dawn, trampling under foot with mad stampings,
shouting curses, howling blasphemies, until weariness finally deadened his fury, and casting himself down upon a furrow, he wept like a child,
thinking that the earth henceforth would be his
real bed, and his only occupation begging in the
streets.

He was awakened by the first rays of the sun
striking his eyes, and the joyful twitter of the
birds which hopped around his head, availing
themselves of the remnants of the nocturnal destruction for their breakfast.

Benumbed with weariness and chilled with the
dampness, he rose from the ground. Pimentó
and his wife were calling him from a distance, in-
viting him to come and take something. Barret

answered them with scorn. Thief! After taking away his shot-gun! And he set out on the
road toward Valencia, trembling with cold, without even knowing where he was going.

He stopped at the tavern of Copa and entered.
Some teamsters of the neighbourhood spoke to
him, expressing sympathy for him in his misfortune, and invited him to have a drink. He accepted gratefully. He craved something which
would counteract this cold, which had penetrated
his very bones. And he who had always been so
sober, drank, one after the other, two glasses
of brandy, which fell into his weakened stomach
like waves of fire.

His face flushed, then became deadly pale; his
eyes grew bloodshot. To the teamsters who
sympathized with him, he seemed expressive and
confiding, almost like one who is happy. He
called them his sons, assuring them that he was
not fretting over so little. Nor had he lost everything. There still remained in his possession the
best thing in his house, the sickle of his grandfather, a jewel which he would not exchange, no,
not for fifty measures of grain.

And from his sash he drew forth the curved
steel, an implement brilliant and pure, of fine

temper and very keen edge, which, as Barret declared, would cut a cigarette-paper in the air.

The teamsters paid up, and urging on their
beasts, set off for Valencia, filling the air with
the creaking of wheels.

The old man stayed in the tavern for more than
an hour, talking to himself, feeling more and
more dizzy, until, made ill at ease by the hard
glances of the landlord, who divined his condition, he experienced a vague feeling of shame,
and set out with unsteady steps without saying
good-bye.

But he was unable to dispel from his mind a
tenacious remembrance. He could see, as he
closed his eyes, a great orchard of oranges which
was about an hour's distance, between Benimaclet and the sea. There he had gone many times
on business, and there he would go now to see if
the devil would be so good as to let him come
across the master, as there was hardly a day that
his avaricious glance did not inspect the beautiful
trees as though he had the oranges counted on
every one.

He arrived after two hours of walking, during
which he stopped many times to balance his body,

which was swaying back and forth upon his unsteady legs.

The brandy had now taken complete possession
of him. He could no longer remember for what
purpose he had come here, so far from that part
of the *huerta* in which his own family lived, and
finally he let himself fall into a field of hemp at
the edge of the road. In a short time, his laboured snores of drunkenness sounded among
the green straight stalks.

When he awoke, the afternoon was well advanced. He felt heavy of head and his stomach
was faint. There was a humming in his ears,
and he had a horrible taste in his coated mouth.
What was he doing here, near the *huerta* of the
Jew? Why had he come so far? His instinctive sense of honour arose; he felt ashamed
at seeing himself in such a state of debasement,
and he tried to get on his feet to go away. The
pressure on his stomach caused by the sickle
which lay crosswise in his sash, gave him chills.

On standing up, he thrust his head out from
among the hemp, and he saw, in a turn of the
road, a little man who was walking slowly along
enveloped in a cape.

Barret felt all his blood suddenly rise to his head; his drunkenness came back on him again. He stood up, tugging at his sickle. And yet they say that the devil is not good? Here was his man; here was the one whom he had been wanting to see since the day before.

The old usurer had hesitated before leaving his house. The affair of old Barret had pricked his conscience; it was a recent event and the *huerta* was treacherous; but the fear that his absence might be taken advantage of in the *huerta* was stronger even than his cowardice, and remembering that the orange estate was distant from the attached farmhouse, he set out on the road.

He was already in sight of the *huerta*, scoffing inwardly at his past fears, when he saw Barret bound out from the plot of cane-brake: like an enormous demon he seemed to him with his red face and extended arms, impeding all flight, cutting him off at the edge of the canal which ran parallel to the road. He thought he must be dreaming; his teeth chattered, his face turned green, and his cape fell off, revealing his old overcoat and the dirty handkerchiefs rolled around his neck. So great was his terror, his agitation, that he spoke to him in Spanish.

"Barret! My son!" he said, in a broken
voice. "The whole thing has been a joke; never
mind. What happened yesterday was only to
make you a little afraid . . . nothing more.
You may stay on your land; come tomorrow to
my house . . . we will talk things over: you
shall pay me whenever you wish."

And he bent backward to avoid the approach
of old Barret: he attempted to sneak away, to
flee from that terrible sickle, upon whose blade a
ray of sun broke, and where the blue of the sky
was reflected. But with the canal behind him,
he could not find a place to retreat, and he threw
himself backward, trying to shield himself with
his clenched hands.

The farmer, showing his sharp white teeth,
smiled like a hyena.

"Thief! thief!" he answered in a voice which
sounded like a snarl.

And waving his weapon from side to side, he
sought for a place where he might strike, avoiding the thin and desperate hands which the miser
held before him.

"But, Barret, my son! what does this mean?
Lower your weapon, do not jest! You are an
honest man . . . think of your daughters! I

repeat to you, it was only a joke.   Come tomorrow and I will give you the key . . . Aaaay!
. . ."

There came a horrible howl; the cry of a wounded beast.   The sickle, tired of encountering obstacles, had lopped off one of the clenched hands at a blow.   It remained hanging by the tendons and the skin, and from the red stump blood spurted violently, spattering Barret, who roared as the hot stream struck his face.

The old man staggered on his legs, but before he fell to the ground the sickle cut horizontally across his neck, and . . . zas! severed the complicated folds of the neckerchief, opening a deep gash which almost separated the head from the trunk.

Don Salvador fell into the canal; his legs remained on the sloping bank, twitching, like a slaughtered steer giving its last kicks.   And meanwhile his head, sunken into the mire, poured out all of his blood through the deep breach, and the waters following their peaceful course with a tranquil murmur which enlivened the solemn silence of the afternoon, became tinged with red.

Barret, stupefied, stood stock still on the shore.

How much blood the old thief had! The canal
grew red, it seemed more copious! Suddenly
the farmer, seized with terror, broke into a run,
as if he feared that the little river of blood would
overflow and drown him.

Before the end of the day, the news had circulated like the report of a cannon which stirred
all the plain. Have you ever seen the hypocritical gesture, the silent rejoicing, with which
a town receives the death of a governor who has
oppressed it? All guessed that it was the hand
of old Barret, yet nobody spoke. The farm-
houses would have opened their last hiding-places
for him; the women would have hidden him
under their skirts.

But the assassin roamed like a madman
through the fields, fleeing from people, lying low
behind the sloping banks, concealing himself
under the little bridges, running across the fields,
frightened by the barking of the dogs, until on
the following day, the rural police surprised him
sleeping in a hayloft.

For six weeks, they talked of nothing in the
huerta but old Barret.

Men and women went on Sundays to the prison
of Valencia as though on a pilgrimage, in order

to look through the bars at the poor liberator, who grew thinner and thinner, his eyes more sunken, and his glance more troubled.

The day of his trial arrived and he was sentenced to death.

The news made a deep impression in the plain; parish priests and mayors started a movement to avoid such a shame. . . . A member of the district to find himself on the scaffold! And as Barret had always been among the docile, voting as the political bosses ordered him to vote, and passively obeying as he was commanded, they made trips to Madrid in order to save his life, and his pardon was opportunely granted.

The farmer came forth from the prison as thin as a mummy, and was conducted to Ceuta, where he died after a few years.

His family scattered; disappearing like a handful of straw in the wind.

The daughters, one after the other, left the families which had taken them in, and went to Valencia to earn their living as servants; and the poor widow, tired of troubling others with her infirmities, was taken to the hospital, and died there in a short time.

The people of the *huerta*, with that facility

which every one displays in forgetting the misfortune of others, scarcely ever spoke of the terrible tragedy of old Barret, and then only to wonder what had become of his daughters.

But nobody forgot the fields and the farmhouse, which remained exactly as on the day when the judge ejected the unfortunate farmer from them.

It was a silent agreement of the whole district; an instinctive conspiracy which few words prepared but in which the very trees and roads seemed to have a part.

Pimentó had given expression to it the very day of the catastrophe. We will see the fine fellow who dares take possession of those lands!

And all the people of the *huerta,* even the women and children, seemed to answer with their glances of mute understanding. Yes; they would see.

The parasitic plants, the thistles, began to spring up from the accursed land which old Barret had stamped upon and cut down with his sickle on that last night, as though he had a presentiment that he would die in prison through its fault.

The sons of Don Salvador, men as rich and

avaricious as their father, cried poverty because this piece of land remained unproductive.

A farmer who lived in another district of the *huerta*, a man who pretended to be a bully and never had enough land, was tempted by their low price, and tackled these fields which inspired fear in all.

He set out to work the land with a gun on his shoulder; he and his farm-hands laughed among themselves at the isolation in which the neighbours left them; the farm-houses were closed to them as they passed, and hostile glances followed from a distance.

The tenant, having the presentiment of an ambush, was vigilant. But his caution served him to no purpose. As he was leaving the fields alone one afternoon, before he had even finished breaking up the ground, two musket-shots were fired at him by some invisible aggressor, and he came forth miraculously uninjured by the handful of birdshot which passed close to his ear.

No one was found in the fields,—not even a fresh foot-print. The sharpshooter had fired from some canal, hidden behind the cane-brake.

With enemies such as these, one has no chance to fight, and on the same night, the Valencian delivered the keys of the farm-house to its masters.

One should have heard the sons of Don Salvador. Was there no law or security for property, . . . nor for anything?

No doubt Pimentó was the instigator of this attack. It was he who was preventing these fields from being cultivated. So the rural police arrested the bully of the *huerta,* and took him off to prison.

But when the moment of taking oath arrived, all of the district filed by before the judge declaring the innocence of Pimentó, and from these cunning rustics not one contradictory word could be forced.

One and all told the same story. Even failing old women who never left their farm-houses declared that on that day, at the very hour when the two reports were heard, Pimentó was in a tavern of Alboraya, enjoying a feast with his friends.

Nothing could be done with these people of imbecile expression and candid looks, who lied with such composure as they scratched the back of their heads. Pimentó was set free, and a sigh of triumph and of satisfaction came from all the houses.

Now the proof was given: now it was known that the cultivation of these lands was paid for with men's lives.

The avaricious masters would not yield. They would cultivate the land themselves. And they sought day-labourers among the long-suffering and submissive people, who, smelling of coarse sheep-wool and poverty, and driven by hunger, descended from the ends of the province, from the mountainous frontiers of Aragon, in search of work.

The *huerta* pitied the poor *churros*.[1] Unfortunate men! They wanted to earn a day's pay; what guilt was theirs? And at night, as they were leaving with their hoes over the shoulder, there was always some good soul to call to them from the door of the tavern of Copa. They made them enter, drink, talked to them confidentially with frowning faces but with the paternal and good-natured tone of one who counsels a child to avoid danger; and the result was that on the following day these docile *churros*, instead of going to the field, presented themselves en masse to the owners of the land.

"Master: we have come to get our pay."

[1] A term of contempt, meaning barbarians.

All the arguments of the two old bachelors, furious at seeing themselves opposed in their avarice, were useless.

"Master," they responded to everything, "we are poor, but we were not born like dogs behind a barn."

And not only did they leave their work, but they passed the warning on to all their countrymen, to avoid earning a day's wages in those fields of Barret's as they would flee from the devil.

The owners of the land even asked for protection in the daily papers. And the rural police went out over the *huerta* in pairs, stopping along the roads to surprise gestures and conversations, but always without results.

Every day they saw the same thing. The women sewing and singing under the vine-arbours; the men bending over in the fields, their eyes upon the ground, their active arms never resting; Pimentó, stretched out like a grand lord under the little wands of bird-lime, waiting for the birds, or torpidly and lazily helping Pepeta; in the tavern of Copa, a few old men, sunning themselves or playing cards. The countryside breathed forth peace, and honourable stolidity;

it was a Moorish Arcadia. But those of the
"*Union*" were on their guard; not a farmer
wanted the land, not even gratuitously; and at
last, the owners had to abandon their undertak-
ing, let the weeds cover the place and the house
fall into decay, while they hoped for the arrival
of some willing man, capable of buying or working the farm.

The *huerta* trembled with satisfaction, seeing
how this wealth was lost, and the heirs of Don
Salvador were being ruined.

It was a new and intense pleasure. Sometimes, after all, the will of the poor must triumph,
and the rich must get the worst of it. And the
hard bread seemed more savoury, the wine better,
the work less burdensome, as they thought of the
fury of the two misers, who with all their money
had to endure the rustics of the *huerta* laughing
at them.

Furthermore, this patch of desolation and
misery in the midst of the *vega*, served to make
the other landlords less exacting. Taking this
neighbourhood as an example, they did not increase their rents and even agreed to wait when
the half year's rent was late in being paid.

Those desolate fields were the talisman which

kept the dwellers of the *huerta* intimately united, in continuous contact: a monument which proᵥ claimed their power over the owners; the miracle of the solidarity of poverty against the laws and the wealth of those who were the lords of the land without working it or sweating over their fields.

All this, which they thought out confusedly, made them believe that on the day when the fields of old Barret should be cultivated, the *huerta* would suffer all manner of misfortunes. And they did not expect, after a triumph of ten years, that any person would dare to enter those abandoned fields except old Tomba, a blind and gibbering shepherd, who in default of an audience daily related his deeds of prowess to his flock of dirty sheep.

Hence the exclamations of astonishment, the gestures of wrath, over all the *huerta*, when Pimentó published the news from field to field, from farmhouse to farmhouse, that the lands of Barret now had a tenant, a stranger, and that he . . . he . . . (whoever he might be), was here with all his family, installing himself without any warning, . . . as if they were his own!

III

WHEN he inspected the uncultivated
land, Batiste told himself that here
he would have work for some time.

Nor did he feel dismayed over the prospect.
He was an energetic, enterprising man, accustomed to working hard to earn a livelihood, and
there was hard work here, and plenty of it, furthermore, he consoled himself by remembering
that he had been even worse off.

His life had been a continuous change of pro-
fession, always within the circle of rural poverty;
but though he had changed his occupation every
year, he had never succeeded in obtaining for his
family the modest comfort which was his only
aspiration.

When he first became acquainted with his wife,
he was a millhand in the neighbourhood of Sagunto. He was then working like a dog (as he
expressed it) to provide for his family; and the
Lord rewarded his labours by sending him every

year a child, all sons,—beautiful creatures who seemed to have been born with teeth, judging by the haste with which they deserted the mother's breast, and began to beg continually for bread.

The result was that in his search for higher wages, he had to give up the mill and become a teamster.

But bad luck pursued him. And yet no one tended the live stock and watched the road as well as he: though nearly dead from fatigue, he had never like his companions dared to sleep in the wagon, letting the beasts, guided by their instinct, find their own way: wakeful at all hours, he always walked beside the nag ahead to avoid the holes and the bad places. Nevertheless, if a wagon upset, it was always his; if an animal fell ill of the rains, it was of course one of Batiste's, in spite of the paternal care with which he hastened to cover the flanks of the horses with trappings of sackcloth, as soon as a few drops had fallen.

During some years of tiresome wanderings over highroads of the province, eating poorly, sleeping in the open, and suffering the torment of passing entire months away from his family, whom he adored with the concentrated affection of a rough and silent man, Batiste experienced only losses, and saw his position getting worse and worse.

His nags died, and he had to go into debt to buy others; the profit that he should have had from the continuous carrying of bags of skin bulged out with wine or oil, would disappear in the hands of hucksters and owners of carts, until the moment arrived when, seeing his impending ruin, he gave up the occupation.

Then he took some land near Sagunto; arid fields, red and eternally thirsty, in which the century-old carob-trees writhed their hollow trunks, and the olive-trees raised their round and dusty heads.

His life was one continuous battle with the drought, an incessant gazing at the sky; whenever a small dark cloud showed itself on the horizon, he trembled with fear.

It rained but little, the crops were bad for four consecutive years, and at last Batiste did not know what to do nor where to turn. Then, in a trip to Valencia, he made the acquaintance of the sons of Don Salvador, excellent gentlemen (the Lord bless them), who offered to let him use these beautiful fields rent-free for two years.

until they could be brought back completely to their old condition.

He had heard rumours of what had happened at the farmhouse; of the causes which had compelled the owner to keep these beautiful lands unproductive; but such a long time had elapsed! Furthermore, poverty has no ears; the fields suited him, and in them he would remain. What did he care for the story of don Salvador and old Barret?

All of which was scorned and forgotten as he looked over the land. And Batiste felt himself filled with sweet ecstasy at finding himself the cultivator of the fertile *huerta*, which he had envied so many times as he passed along the highroad of Valencia to Sagunto.

This was fine land; always green; of inexhaustible fertility, producing one harvest after another; the red water circulating at all hours like life-giving blood through the innumerable canals and irrigation trenches which furrowed its surface like a complicated network of veins and arteries; so fertile that entire families were supported by patches so small that they looked like green handkerchiefs. The dry fields off there near Sagunto reminded him of an inferno of drought, from which he fortunately had liberated himself.

Now he was sure that he was on the right road. To work! The fields were ruined; there was much work to be done; but when one is so willing! And this big, robust, muscular fellow, with the shoulders of a giant, closely cropped round head, and good-natured countenance supported by the heavy neck of a monk, extended his powerful arms, accustomed to raising sacks of flour and the heavy skin sacks of the teamster's trade, aloft in the air, and stretched himself.

He was so absorbed in his lands that he scarcely noticed the curiosity of his neighbours.

Restless heads appeared between the canebrake; men, stretched out at full-length on the sloping banks, were watching him; even the women and the children of the adjoining *huertas* followed his movements.

Batiste did not mind them. It was curiosity, the hostile expectation which recent arrivals always inspire. Well did he know what that was; they would get accustomed to it. Furthermore, perhaps they were interested in seeing how that desolate growth burned, which ten years of abandonment had heaped upon the fields of Barret.

And aided by his wife and children, he went about on the day after his arrival, burning up all the parasitic vegetation.

The shrubs writhed in the flames; they fell like live coals from whose ashes the loathsome vermin escaped all singed, and the farmhouse seemed lost amid the clouds of smoke from these fires, which awakened silent anger in all the *huerta*.

The fields once cleared, Batiste without losing time proceeded to cultivate them. They were somewhat hard; but like an expert farmer, he planned to work them little by little, in sections, and marking out a plot near his farmhouse, he began to break up the earth, aided by all his family.

The neighbours made sport of them with an irony which betrayed their irritation. A pretty family! They were gipsies, like those who sleep under the bridges. They lived in that old farmhouse like shipwrecked sailors who are holding out in a ruined boat; plugging a hole here, shoring there, doing real wonders to sustain the straw roof, and distributing their poor furniture, carefully polished, in all the rooms which had been before the burrowing place of rats and vermin.

In their industry, they were like a nest of squirrels, unable to keep idle while the father was working. Teresa, the wife, and Roseta, the eldest daughter, with their skirts tucked in between their legs, and hoe in hand, dug with more zeal than day-labourers, resting only to throw back the locks of hair which kept straggling over their red, perspiring foreheads. The eldest son made continuous trips to Valencia with the rush-basket on his shoulder, carrying manure and rubbish which he piled up in two heaps like columns of honour at the entrance to the farmhouse; and the three little tots, grave and laborious, as if they understood the situation of the family, went down on all fours behind the diggers, tearing up the hard roots of the burned shrubs from the earth.

This preparatory work lasted more than a week, the family sweating and panting from dawn till night.

Half of the land having been broken up, Batiste fenced in the plot and tilled it with the aid of the willing nag, which was like one of the family.

He had only to proceed to cultivate. They were then in Saint Martin's summer, the time of

sowing, and the labourer divided the broken-up
earth into three parts. The greater part was for
wheat, a smaller patch for beans, and another
part for fodder, for it would not do to forget
Morrut, the dear old horse: well had he earned
it.

And with the joy of those who discover a port
after a hard voyage, the family proceeded to the
sowing. The future was assured. The fields of
the *huerta* never failed; here bread for all the
year would be forthcoming.

On the afternoon which completed the sowing,
they saw coming over the adjoining road some
sheep with dirty wool, which stopped timidly at
the end of the field.

Behind them walked an old man, like dried up
parchment, yellowish, with deep sunken eyes and
a mouth surrounded by a circle of wrinkles.
He was walking with firm steps, but with his
shepherd's crook ahead of him, as though feeling
his way along the road.

The family looked at him with attention; he
was the only person who had ventured to approach the land within the two weeks they were
here. On noticing the hesitation of the sheep,
he shouted to them to go on.

Batiste went out to meet the old man; he could not pass through; the fields were now under cultivation. Did he not know?

Old Tomba had heard something, but during the two preceding weeks, he had taken out his flock to graze upon the rank grass in the ravine of Carraixet, without concerning himself about the fields. So indeed they now were cultivated?

And the old shepherd raised his head, and with his almost sightless eyes made an effort to see the bold man who dared to do that which was held to be impossible in all the *huerta*.

He was silent for a long while. Then at last he began to mutter sadly: Too bad. He had also been daring in his youth; he had liked to go counter to everything. But when the enemies are so many! Very bad! He had put himself into an awkward position. These lands, since the time of old Barret, had been accursed. He could take his, Tomba's, word for it; he was old and experienced; they would bring him misfortune.

And the shepherd called his flock and made them start out again along the road, but before departing, he threw back his cloak, raised his emaciated arms, and with a certain intonation characteristic of a seer who forecasts the future, or of a prophet who scents disaster, he cried to Batiste:

"Believe me, my son, they will bring you misfortune!"

This encounter gave the *huerta* another cause for anger.

Old Tomba could not bring his sheep back into those lands, after enjoying the peaceful use of their fodder for ten years!

Not a word was said as to the legitimacy of the refusal, inasmuch as the land was now under cultivation; they spoke only of the respect which the old shepherd deserved, a man who in his youth had "eaten up" the French alive, who had seen much of the world, and whose wisdom, demonstrated by half-spoken words and incoherent advice, inspired a superstitious respect among the people of the *huerta*.

After Batiste and his family saw the bosom of the earth well-filled with fertile seed, they began, for lack of work more pressing, to think of the house.   The fields would do their duty; now the time had arrived to think about themselves.

And for the first time since his coming to the *huerta*, Batiste left his land for Valencia to load into his cart all the rubbish of the city which might be useful to him.

This man was like a lucky ant. The mounds started by Batiste increased considerably with the expeditions of the father. The heap of manure which formed a defensive screen before the farmhouse, grew rapidly, and beyond, there was piling up a mound of hundreds of broken bricks, worm-eaten wood, broken-down doors, windows reduced to splinters, all the refuse of the demolished buildings of the city.

The people of the *huerta* looked with astonishment at the dispatch and clever skill of these laborious ants as they worked to prepare their home.

The straw roof of the house stood erect again; some of the rafters of the roof, corroded by the rains, were reinforced, others substituted. A new layer of straw now covered the two hanging planes of the exterior; even the little crosses at the ends were supplanted by others which Batiste had daintily made with his clasp knife, decorating their corners with notched grooves: and in all the neighbourhood, there was not a roof which rose more trimly.

The neighbours, on noticing how Barret's house was improved when the roof was placed erect, saw in it something to mock and to challenge.

Then the work below was started. What ways and means of utilizing the rubbish of Valencia! The chinks disappeared, and the plastering of the walls being finished, the wife and daughters white-washed them a dazzling white. The door, new and painted blue, seemed to be the mother of all the little windows, which showed their four square faces of the same colour through the openings of the walls; under the vine-arbour, Batiste made a little enclosure paved with red bricks, so the women might sew there during the afternoon. The well, after a week of descents and laborious carryings, was cleared of all the rocks and the refuse with which the rascals of the *huerta* had filled it for the last ten years, and its water, fresh and clear, began to rise once more in the mossy bucket, with joyful creakings of the pulley, which seemed to laugh at the district with the strident peals of laughter of a malicious old woman.

The neighbours chocked down their fury in silence. Thief! More than thief! A fine way to work! This man, in his robust arms, seemed to possess two magic wands that transformed all that he touched!

Two months had passed since his arrival, yet he had not left his land a half-dozen times; he was always there, his head between his shoulders, intoxicated with work. And the house of Barret began to present a smiling and coquettish aspect, such as it had never possessed in the days of its former master.

The corral, previously enclosed with rotting cane-brake, now had sides of pickets and clay painted white, along whose edges strutted the ruddy hens, and the cock, excited, shook his red comb. In the little square in front of the house, beds of morning-glories and climbing plants blossomed; a row of chipped jars painted blue served as flower-pots on the bench of red bricks; and through the half-open door, oh vain fellow! the new pitcher-shelf might be seen, with its enamelled tiling, and its glazed green pitchers, casting insolent reflections which blinded the eyes of the passerby who went along the adjoining road.

All the *huerta* with increasing fury ran to Pimentó. "Could it possibly be permitted?

What did the terrible husband of Pepeta think of doing?"

And Pimentó, scratching his forehead, listened to them with a certain confusion.

What was he going to do? He would say just two little words to this stranger who had set himself to cultivate that which was not his; he would give him a hint, a very serious hint, not to be a fool, but to let the land go, as he had no business there. But that accursed man would not come forth from his fields, and it would never do to go to him and threaten him in his own house. It would mean the giving of a foundation for that which must follow. He had to be cautious and watch till he came out. In short, a little patience. He was able to assure them that the man in question would not reap the wheat, nor gather the beans, nor anything which had been planted in the fields of Barret. That should be for the devil.

Pimentó's words calmed the neighbours, who followed the progress of the accursed family with attentive glances, wishing silently that the hour of their ruin would soon arrive.

One afternoon, Batiste returned from Valencia very well pleased with the result of his trip.

He wanted no idle hands in his house. Batiste, when the work in the field did not take his time, was occupied in going to the city for manure. The little girl, a willing youngster, who once they were settled was of small use at home, had, thanks to the patronage of the sons of Don Salvador, who seemed very well satisfied with his new tenant, just succeeded in getting taken into a silk factory.

On the following day, Roseta would be one of the string of girls who, awakening with the dawn, marched with waving skirts and their little baskets on their arm, over all the paths, on their way to the city to spin the silky cocoon with the thick fingers of the daughters of the *huerta*.

When Batiste arrived near the tavern of Copa, a man appeared in the road, emerging from an adjoining path, and walked slowly toward him, giving him to understand that he desired to speak to him.

Batiste stopped, regretting inwardly that he did not have with him so much as a clasp knife or a hoe; but calm and quiet, he raised his round head with the imperious expression so much feared by his family and crossed his muscular arms, the arms of a former millhand, on his breast.

He knew this man, although he had never spoken with him; it was Pimentó.

The meeting which he had dreaded so much finally occurred.

The bully measured this odious intruder with a glance, and spoke to him in a bland voice, striving to give an accent of good-natured counsel to his ferocity and evil intention.

He wished to say to him just two words: he had been wanting to do so for some time, but how? did he never come forth from his land?

Two little words, no more.

And he gave him the couple of words, counselling him to leave the lands of old Barret as soon as possible. He should believe the people who wished him well, those who knew the *huerta*. His presence there was an offence, and the farmhouse, which was almost new, was an insult to the poor people. He ought to believe him, and with his family go away to other parts.

Batiste smiled ironically on hearing Pimentó, who seemed confused by the serenity of the intruder, humbled by meeting a man who did not seem afraid of him.

Go away?   There was not a bully in all the *huerta* who could make him abandon that which was now his; that which was watered by his sweat; moreover he had to earn bread for his family.   He was a peaceful man, understand! but if they trifled with him, he had just as much manly spirit as most.   Let every one attend to his own business, for he thought that he would do enough if he attended to his own, and failed nobody.

And scornfully turning his back upon the Valencian, he went his way.

Pimentó, accustomed to making all the *huerta* tremble, was more and more disconcerted by the serenity of Batiste.

"Is that your last word?" he shouted to him when he was already at some distance.

"Yes, the last," answered Batiste without turning.

And he went ahead, disappearing in a curve of the road.   At some distance, on the old farm of Barret, the dog was barking, scenting the approach of his master.

On finding himself alone, Pimentó again recovered his arrogance.   *Cristo!*   How this old fellow had mocked him!   He muttered some

curses, and clenching his fist, shook it threaten-
ingly at the bend in the road where Batiste had
disappeared.

"You shall pay for this,—you shall pay for
this, you thug!"

In his tone which trembled with madness,
there vibrated all the condensed hatred of the
huerta.

IV

I T was Thursday, and according to a custom which dated back for five centuries, the Tribunal of the Waters was going to meet at the doorway of the Cathedral named after the Apostles.

The clock of the Miguelete pointed to a little after ten, and the inhabitants of the *huerta* were gathering in idle groups or seating themselves about the large basin of the dry fountain which adorned the *plaza*, forming about its base an animated wreath of blue and white cloaks, red and yellow handkerchiefs, and skirts of calico prints of bright colours.

Others were arriving, drawing up their horses, with their rush-baskets loaded with manure, satisfied with the collection they had made in the streets; still others, in empty carts, were trying to persuade the police to allow their vehicles to remain there; and while the old folks chatted with the women, the young went into the neighbouring café, to kill time over a glass of brandy, while chewing at a three-centime cigar.

All those of the *huerta* who had grievances to avenge were here, gesticulating and scowling, speaking of their rights, impatient to let loose the interminable chain of their complaints before the syndics or judges of the seven canals.

The bailiff of the tribunal, who had been carrying on this contest with the insolent and aggressive crowd for more than fifty years, placed a long sofa of old damask which was on its last legs within the shadow of the Gothic portal, and then set up a low railing, thereby closing in the square of sidewalk which had to serve the purpose of an audience-chamber.

The portal of the Apostles, old, reddish, corroded by the centuries, extending its gnawed beauty to the light of the sun, formed a background worthy of an ancient tribunal; it was like a canopy of stone devised to protect an institution five centuries old.

In the tympanum appeared the Virgin with six angels, with stiff white gowns and wings of fine plumage, chubby-cheeked, with heavy curls and flaming tufts of hair, playing violas and flutes, flageolets and tambourines. Three garlands of little figures, angels, kings, and saints, covered with openwork canopies, ran through three arches superposed over the three portals. In the thick, solid walls, forepart of the portal, the twelve apostles might be seen, but so disfigured, so ill-treated, that Jesus himself would not have known them; the feet gnawed, the nostrils broken, the hands mangled; a line of huge figures who, rather than apostles, looked like sick men who had escaped from a clinic, and were sorrowfully displaying their shapeless stumps. Above, at the top of the portal, there opened out like a gigantic flower covered with wire netting, the coloured rose-window which admitted light to the church; and on the lower part the stone along the base of the columns adorned with the shields of Aragon, was worn, the corners and foliage having become indistinct through the rubbing of innumerable generations.

By this erosion of the portals the passing of riot and revolt might be divined. A whole people had met and mingled beside these stones; here, in other centuries, the turbulent Valencian populace, shouting and red with fury, had moved about; and the saints of the portal, muti-

lated and smooth as Egyptian mummies, gazing
at the sky with their broken heads, appeared to
be still listening to the Revolutionary bell of
the Union, or the arquebus shots of the Broth-
erhood.

The bailiff finished arranging the Tribunal,
and placed himself at the entrance of the enclosure to await the judges. The latter arrived
solemnly, dressed in black, with white sandals,
and silken handkerchiefs under their broad hats,
they had the appearance of rich farmers. Each
was followed by a cortège of canal-guards, and
by persistent supplicants who, before the hour
of justice, were seeking to predispose the judges'
minds in their favour.

The farmers gazed with respect at these
judges, come forth from their own class, whose
deliberations did not admit of any appeal.
They were the masters of the water: in their
hands remained the living of the families, the
nourishment of the fields, the timely watering,
the lack of which kills a harvest. And the
people of these wide plains, separated by the
river, which is like an impassable frontier,
designated the judges by the number of the
canals.

A little, thin, bent, old man, whose red and horny hands trembled as they rested on the thick staff, was Cuart de Faitanar; the other, stout and imposing, with small eyes scarcely visible under bushy white brows, was Mislata. Soon Roscaña arrived; a youth who wore a blouse that had been freshly ironed, and whose head was round. After these appeared in sequence the rest of the seven:—Favara, Robella, Tornos and Mestalla.

Now all the representatives of the four plains were there; the one on the left bank of the river; the one with the four canals; the one which the *huerta* of Rufaza encircles with its roads of luxuriant foliage ending at the confines of the marshy Albufera; and the plain on the right bank of the Turia, the poetic one, with its strawberries of Benimaclet, its *cyperus* of Alboraya and its gardens always overrun with flowers.

The seven judges saluted, like people who had not seen each other for a week; they spoke of their business beside the door of the Cathedral: from time to time, upon opening the wooden screens covered with religious advertisements, a puff of incense-laden air, somewhat like the damp exhalation from a subter-

ranean cavern, diffused itself into the burning
atmosphere of the *plaza*.

At half-past eleven, when the divine offices
were ended and only some belated devotee was
still coming from the temple, the Tribunal began
to operate.

The seven judges seated themselves on the
old sofa; then the people of the *huerta* came
running up from all sides of the *plaza*, to gather
around the railing, pressing their perspiring bodies, which smelled of straw and coarse sheep's
wool, close together, and the bailiff, rigid and
majestic, took his place near the pole topped with
a bronze crook, symbolic of aquatic majesty.

The seven syndics removed their hats and remained with their hands between the knees and
their eyes upon the ground, while the eldest pronounced the customary sentence:

"Let the Tribunal begin."

Absolute stillness. The crowd, observing religious silence, seemed here, in the midst of the
plaza, to be worshipping in a temple. The
sound of carriages, the clatter of tramways, all
the din of modern life passed by, without touching or stirring this most ancient institution,
which remained tranquil, like one who finds him-

self in his own house, insensible to time, paying no attention to the radical change surrounding it, incapable of any reform.

The inhabitants of the *huerta* were proud of their tribunal. It dispensed justice; the penalty without delay, and nothing done with papers, which confuse and puzzle honest men.

The absence of stamped paper and of the clerk of court who terrifies, was the part best liked by these people who were accustomed to looking upon the art of writing of which they were ignorant with a certain superstitious terror. Here were no secretary, no pens, no days of anxiety while awaiting sentence, no terrifying guards, nor anything more than words.

The judges kept the declarations in their memory, and passed sentence immediately with the tranquillity of those who know that their decisions must be fulfilled. On him who would be insolent with the tribunal, a fine was imposed; from him who had refused to comply with the verdict, the water was taken away forever, and he must die of hunger.

Nobody played with this tribunal. It was the simple patriarchal justice of the good legendary king, coming forth mornings to the door of his palace in order to settle the disputes of his subjects; the judicial system of the Kabila chief, passing sentences at his tent-entrance. Thus are rascals punished, and the honourable triumph, and there is peace.

And the public, men, women, and children, fearful of missing a word, pressed close together against the railing, moving, sometimes, with violent contortions of their shoulders, in order to escape from suffocation.

The complainants would appear at the other side of the railing, before the sofa as old as the tribunal itself.

The bailiff would take away their staffs and shepherds' crooks, which he regarded as offensive arms incompatible with the respect due the tribunal. He pushed them forward until with their mantle folded over their hands they were planted some paces distant from the judges, and if they were slow in baring their head, the handkerchief was wrested from it with two tugs. It was hard, but with this crafty people it was necessary to act thus.

The line filing by brought a continuous outburst of intricate questions, which the judges settled with marvellous facility.

The keepers of the canals and the irrigation-guards, charged with the establishment of each one's turn in the irrigation, formulated their charges, and the defendants appeared to defend themselves with arguments. The old men allowed their sons, who knew how to express themselves with more energy, to speak; the widow appeared, accompanied by some friend of the deceased, a devoted protector, who acted as her spokesman.

The passion of the south cropped out in every case.

In the midst of the accusation, the defendant would not be able to contain himself. "You lie! What you say is evil and false! You are trying to ruin me!"

But the seven judges received these interruptions with furious glances. Here nobody was permitted to speak before his own turn came. At the second interruption, he would have to pay a fine of so many *sous*. And he who was obstinate, driven by his vehement madness, which would not permit him to be silent before the accuser, paid more and more *sous*.

The judges, without giving up their seats, would put their heads together like playful

goats, and whisper together for some seconds;
then the eldest, in a composed and solemn voice,
pronounced the sentence, designating the fine in
sous and pounds, as if money had suffered no
change, and majestic Justice with its red robe
and its escort of plumed crossbowmen were still
passing through the centre of the *plaza*.

It was after twelve, and the seven judges were
beginning to show signs of being weary of such
prodigious outpouring of the stream of justice,
when the bailiff called out loudly to Bautista Borrull, denouncing him for infraction and disobe-
dience of irrigation-rights.

Pimentó and Batiste passed the railing, and
the people pressed up even closer against the
bar.

Here were many of those who lived near the
ancient land of Barret.

This trial was interesting. The hated new-
comer had been denounced by Pimentó, who was
the *"atandador"* [1] of that district.

The bully, by mixing up in elections, and
strutting about like a fighting cock all over the
neighbourhood, had won this office which gave
him a certain air of authority and strengthened

[1] One in charge of the *tanda,* or turn in irrigating.

his prestige among the neighbours, who made much of him and treated him on irrigation days.

Batiste was amazed at this unjust denunciation. His pallor was that of indignation. He gazed with eyes full of fury at all the familiar mocking faces, which were pressing against the rail, and at his enemy Pimentó, who was strutting about proudly, like a man accustomed to appearing before the tribunal, and to whom a small part of its unquestionable authority belonged.

"Speak," said the eldest of the judges, putting one foot forward, for according to a century-old custom, the tribunal, instead of using the hands, signalled with the white sandal to him who should speak.

Pimentó poured forth his accusation. This man who was beside him, perhaps because he was new in the *huerta*, seemed to think that the apportionment of the water was a trifling matter, and that he could suit his own blessed will.

He, Pimentó, the *atandador*, who represented the authority of the canals in his district, had set for Batiste the hour for watering his wheat. It was two o'clock in the morning. But doubtless the señor, not wishing to arise at that hour, had let his turn go, and at five, when the water was intended for others, he had raised the flood-gate without permission from anybody (the *first* offence), and attempted to water his fields, resolving to oppose, by main force, the orders of the *atandador,* which constituted the *third* and last offence.

The thrice-guilty delinquent, turning all the colours of the rainbow, and indignant at the words of Pimentó, was not able to restrain himself.

"You lie, and lie doubly!"

The tribunal became indignant at the heat and the lack of respect with which this man was protesting.

If he did not keep silent he would be fined.

But what was a fine for the concentrated wrath of a peaceful man! He kept on protesting against the injustice of men, against the tribunal which had, as its servants, such rogues and liars as Pimentó.

The tribunal was stirred up; the seven judges became excited.

Four *sous* for a fine!

Batiste, realizing his situation, suddenly grew

silent, terrified at having incurred a fine, while laughter came from the crowd and howls of joy from his enemies.

He remained motionless, with bowed head, and his eyes dimmed with tears of rage, while his brutal enemy finished formulating his denunciation.

"Speak," the tribunal said to him. But little sympathy was noted in the looks of the judges for this disturber, who had come to trouble the solemnity of their deliberations with his protests.

Batiste, trembling with rage, stammered, not knowing how to begin his defence because of the very fact that it seemed to him perfectly just.

The court had been misled; Pimentó was a liar and furthermore his declared enemy. He had told him that his time for irrigation came at five, he remembered it very well, and was now affirming that it was two; just to make him incur a fine, to destroy the wheat upon which the life of his family depended. . . . Did the tribunal value the word of an honest man? Then this was the truth, although he was not able to present witnesses. It seemed impossible that the honourable syndics, all good people, should trust a rascal like Pimentó!

The white sandal of the president struck the square tile of the sidewalk, as if to avert the storm of protests and the lack of respect which he saw from afar.

"Be silent."

And Batiste was silent, while the seven-headed monster, folding itself up again on the sofa of damask, was whispering, preparing the sentence.

"The tribunal decrees . . ." said the eldest judge, and there was absolute silence.

All the people around the roped space showed a certain anxiety in their eyes, as if they were the sentenced. They were hanging on the lips of the eldest judge.

"Batiste Borrull shall pay two pounds for a penalty, and four *sous* for a fine."

A murmur of satisfaction arose and spread, and one old woman even began to clap her hands, shouting "Hurrah! hurrah!" amid the loud laughter of the people.

Batiste went out blindly from the tribunal, with his head lowered as though he were about to fight, and Pimentó prudently stayed behind.

If the people had not parted, opening the way,

for him, it is certain that he would have struck out with his powerful fists, and given the hostile rabble a beating on the spot.

He departed. He went to the house of his masters to tell them of what had happened, of the ill will of this people, pledged to embitter his existence for him; and an hour later, already more composed by the kind words of the *señores*, he set forth on the road toward his home.

Insufferable torment! Marching close to their carts loaded with manure or mounted on their donkeys above the empty hampers, he kept meeting on the low road of Alboraya many of those who had been present at the trial.

They were hostile people, neighbours whom he never greeted.

When he passed beside them, they remained silent, and made an effort to keep their gravity, although a malicious joy glowed in their eyes; but as soon as he had gone by, they burst into insolent laughter behind his back, and he even heard the voice of a lad who shouted, mimicking the grave tone of the president:

"Four *sous* for a fine!"

In the distance he saw, in the doorway of the tavern of Copa, his enemy Pimentó, with an earthen jug in hand, in the midst of a circle of friends, gesticulating and laughing as if he were imitating the protests and complaints of the one denounced. His sentence was the theme of rejoicing for the *huerta:* all were laughing.

God! Now he, a man of peace and a kind father, understood why it is that men kill.

His powerful arms trembled, and he felt a cruel itching in the hands. He slackened his pace on approaching the house of Copa; he wanted to see whether they would mock him to his face.

He even thought, a strange novelty, of entering for the first time to drink a glass of wine face to face with his enemies; but the two pound fine lay heavy on his heart and he repented of his generosity. This was a conspiracy against the footwear of his sons; it would take all the little pile of farthings hoarded together by Teresa to buy new sandals for the little ones.

As he passed the front of the tavern, Pimentó hid with the excuse of filling the jug, and his friends pretended not to see Batiste.

His aspect of a man ready for anything inspired respect in his neighbours.

But this triumph filled him with sadness.

How hateful the people were to him!   The entire *vega* arose before him, scowling and threatening at all hours.   This was not living.   Even
in the daytime, he avoided coming out of his
fields, shunning all contact with his neighbours.

He did not fear them, but like a prudent man,
avoided disputes.

At night, he slept restlessly, and many times,
at the slightest barking of the dogs, he leaped
out of bed, rushed from the house, shotgun in
hand, and even believed on more than one oc-
casion that he saw black forms which fled among
the adjoining paths.

He feared for his harvest, for the wheat which
was the hope of the family and whose growth
was followed in silence but with envious glances
from the other farmhouses.

He knew of the threats of Pimentó, who supported by all the *huerta*, swore that this wheat
should not be cut by him who had sowed it, and
Batiste almost forgot his sons in thinking about
his fields, of the series of green waves which
grew and grew under the rays of the sun and
which must turn into golden piles of ripe wheat.

The silent and concentrated hatred followed
him out upon the road.   The women drew away,

with curling lips, and did not deign to salute
him, as is the custom in the *huerta;* the men who
were working in the fields adjoining the road,
called to each other with insolent expressions
which were directed indirectly at Batiste; and
the little children shouted from a distance,
"Thug! Jew!" without adding more to such insults, as if they alone were applicable to the
enemy of the *huerta.*

Ah! If he had not had the fists of a giant,
those enormous shoulders and that expression of
a man who has few friends, how soon the entire
vega would have settled with him! Each one
hoping that the other would be the first to dare,
they contented themselves with insulting him
from a distance.

Batiste, in the midst of the sadness which this
solitude inspired in him, experienced one slight
satisfaction. Already close to the farmhouse,
when he heard the barkings of the dog who had
scented his approach, he saw a boy, an overgrown youth, seated on a sloping bank with the
sickle between his legs, and holding some piles
of cut brushwood at his side, who stood up to
greet him.

"Good day, Señor Batiste!"

And the salutation, the trembling voice of a timid boy with which he spoke to him, impressed him pleasantly.

The friendliness of this child was a small matter, yet he experienced the impression of a feverish man upon feeling the coolness of water.

He gazed with tenderness at the blue eyes, the smiling face covered by a coat of down, and searched his memory as to who the boy might be. Finally he remembered that he was the grandson of old Tomba, the blind shepherd whom all the *huerta* respected; a good boy who was serving as a servant to a butcher at Alboraya, whose herd the old man tended.

"Thanks, little one, thanks," he murmured, acknowledging the salute.

And he went ahead, and was welcomed by his dog, who leaped before him, and rubbed himself against his corduroy trousers.

In the door of the cabin stood his wife surrounded by the little ones, waiting impatiently, for the supper hour had already passed.

Batiste looked at the fields, and all the fury he had suffered an hour ago before the Tribunal of the Waters, returned at a stroke and like a furious wave flooded his consciousness.

His wheat was thirsty. He had only to see it;
its leaves shrivelled, the green colour, before so
lustrous, now of a yellow transparency. The
irrigation had failed him; the turn of which
Pimentó, with his sly and evil tricks, had robbed
him, would not belong to him until fifteen days
had passed, because the water was scarce; and on
top of this misfortune all that damned string of
pounds and *sous* for a fine. Christ!

He ate without any appetite, telling his wife
the while of the occurrence at the Tribunal.

Poor Teresa listened to her husband, pale
with the emotion of the countrywoman who feels
a pang in her heart when there must be a loosening of the knot of the stocking which guards the
money in the bottom of the chest. Sovereign
queen! They had determined to ruin them!
What sorrow at the evening-meal!

And letting her spoon fall into the frying-pan
of rice, she wept, swallowing her tears. Then
she became red with sudden passion, looked out
at the expanse of plain with she saw in front
of her door, with its white farmhouses and its
waves of green, and stretching out her arms, she
cried: "Rascals! Rascals!"

The little folks, frightened by their father's

scowl, and the cries of their mother, were afraid
to eat. They looked from one to the other with
indecision and wonder, picked at their noses
to be doing something, and all of them ended by
imitating their mother and weeping over the
rice.

Batiste, agitated by the chorus of sobs, arose
furiously, and almost kicked over the little table
as he flung himself out of the house.

What an afternoon! The thirst of his wheat
and the remembrance of the fine were like two
fierce dogs tearing at his heart. When one, tired
of biting him, was going to sleep, the other arrived at full speed and fixed his teeth in him.

He wanted to distract his thoughts, to forget
himself in work, and he gave himself over with
all his will to the task he had in hand, a pigsty
which he was putting up in the corral.

But the work did not progress. He was suffocating between the mud-walls; he wanted to look
at the fields, he was like those who feel the need
to look upon their misfortune, to yield utterly
and drink the cup of sorrow to the dregs. And
with his hands full of clay, he came out from
the farm-yard, and remained standing before
the oblong patch of shrivelled wheat.

A few steps away, at the edge of the road, the murmuring canal brimmed with red water ran by.

The life-giving blood of the *huerta* was flowing far away, for other fields whose masters did not have the misfortune of being hated; and here was his poor wheat, shrivelled, languishing, bowing its green head as if it were making signs to the water to come near and caress it with its cool kiss.

To poor Batiste, it seemed that the sun was burning hotter than on other days. The sun was at the horizon, yet the poor man imagined that its rays were vertical, and that everything was burning up.

His land was cracking open, it parted in tortuous grooves, forming a thousand mouths which vainly awaited a swallow of water.

Nor would the wheat hold its thirst until the next irrigation. It would die, it would become dried up, the family would not have bread; and besides so much misery, a fine on top of everything. And people even find fault if men go to ruin!

Furious he walked back and forth along the border of his oblong plot. Ah, Pimentó!

Greatest of scoundrels! If there were no Civil Guards!

And like shipwrecked mariners, agonizing with hunger and thirst, who in their delirium see only interminable banquet-tables, and the clearest springs, Batiste confusedly saw fields of wheat whose stalks were green and straight, and the water entering, gushing from the mouths of the sloping-banks, extending itself with a luminous rippling, as if it laughed softly at feeling the tickling of the thirsty earth.

At the sinking of the sun, Batiste felt a certain relief, as though it had gone out forever, and his harvest was saved.

He went away from his fields, from his farmhouse, and unconsciously, with slow steps, took the road below, toward the tavern of Copa. The thought of the rural police had left his mind, and he accepted the possibility of a meeting with Pimentó, who should not be very far away from the tavern, with a certain feeling of pleasure.

Along the borders of the road, there were coming toward him swift rows of girls, hamper on arm, and skirts flying, returning from the factories of the city.

Blue shadows were spreading over the *huerta*;

in the background, over the darkening mountains, the clouds were growing red with the
splendour of some far distant fire; in the direction of the sea, the first stars were trembling in
the infinite blue; the dogs were barking mourn-
fully; and with the monotonous singing of the
frogs and the crickets, was mingled the confused
creaking of invisible wagons, departing over all
the roads of the immense plain.

Batiste saw his daughter coming, separated
from all the girls, walking with slow steps. But
not alone. It seemed to him that she was talking with a man who followed in the same direction as herself, although somewhat apart, as
the betrothed always walk in the *huerta*, for
whom approach is a sign of sin.

When he saw Batiste in the middle of the
road, the man slackened his pace and remained
at a distance as Roseta approached her father.

The latter remained motionless, as he wanted
the stranger to advance so that he might recog-
nize him.

"Good night, Señor Batiste."

It was the same timid voice which had saluted him at midday. The grandson of old
Tomba. That scamp seemed to have nothing to

do but wander over the roads, and greet him, and thrust himself before his eyes with his bland sweetness.

He looked at his daughter, who grew red under the gaze, and lowered her eyes.

"Go home; home, . . . I will settle with you!"

And with all the terrible majesty of the Latin father, the absolute master of his children, and more inclined to inspire fear than affection, he started after the tremulous Roseta, who, as she drew near the farm, anticipated a sure cudgeling.

She was mistaken. At that moment the poor father had no other children in the world but his crops, the poor sick wheat, shrivelling, drying, and crying out to him, begging for a swallow in order not to die.

And of this he thought while his wife was getting the supper ready. Roseta was bustling about pretending to be busy, in order not to attract attention and expecting from one moment to the next an outburst of terrible anger. But Batiste, seated before the little dwarfish table, surrounded by all the young people of his family, who were gazing greedily by the candle-light at the earthenware dish, filled with

smoking hake and potatoes, went on thinking of
his fields.

The woman was still sighing, pondering the
fine; making comparisons, without doubt, between the fabulous sum which they were going
to wrest from her, and the ease with which the
entire family were eating.

Batiste, contemplating the voracity of his children, scarcely ate. Batistet, the eldest son, even
appropriated with feigned abstraction of the
pieces of bread belonging to the little ones. To
Roseta, fear gave a fierce appetite.

Never until then did Batiste comprehend the
load which was weighing upon his shoulders.
These mouths which opened to swallow up the
meagre savings of the family would be without
food if that land outside should dry.

And all for what? On account of the injustice of men, because there are laws made to mo-
lest honest workmen. . . . He should not stand
this. His family before everything else. Did
he not feel capable of defending his own from
even greater dangers? Did he not owe them the
duty of maintaining them? He was capable of
becoming a thief in order to give them food.
Why then, did he have to submit, when he was

not trying to steal, but to give life to his crops, which were all his own?

The image of the canal, which at a short distance was dragging along its murmuring supply for others, was torturing him. It enraged him that life should be passing by at his very door without his being able to profit by it, because the laws wished it so.

Suddenly he arose, like a man who has adopted a resolution and who in order to fulfil it, stamps everything under foot.

"To irrigate!   To irrigate!"

The woman was terrified, for she quickly guessed all the danger of the desperate resolution.   For Heaven's sake, Batiste! . . . They would impose upon him a greater fine; perhaps the Tribunal, offended by his rebellion, would take the water away from him forever!   He ought to consider it. . . . It was better to wait.

But Batiste had the enduring wrath of phlegmatic and slow men, who, when they once lose their composure, are slow to recover it.

"Irrigate!   Irrigate!"

And Batistet, gaily repeating the words of his father, picked up the large hoes, and started from the house, followed by his sister and the little ones.

They all wished to take part in this work, which seemed like a holiday.

The family felt the exhilaration of a people which, by a revolution, recovers its liberty.

They approached the canal, which was murmuring in the shade. The immense plain was lost in the blue shadow, the cane-brake undulated in dark and murmuring masses, and the stars twinkled in the heavens.

Batiste went into the canal knee-deep, lowering the gates which held the water, while his son, his wife and even his daughter attacked the sloping banks with the hoes, opening gaps, through which the water gushed.

All the family felt a sensation of coolness and of well-being.

The earth sung merrily with a greedy glu-glu, which touched the heart. "Drink, drink, poor thing!" And their feet sank in the mud, as bent over they went from one side to the other of the field, looking to see if the water had reached every part.

Batiste muttered with the cruel satisfaction

which the joy of the prohibited produces. What a load was lifted from him! The Tribunal might come now, and do whatever it wished. His field had drunk; this was the main thing.

And as with the acute hearing of a man accustomed to the solitude, he thought that he perceived a certain strange noise in the neighbouring cane-brake, he ran to the farm, and returned immediately, holding a new shotgun.

With the weapon over his arm, and his finger on the trigger, he stood more than an hour close to the bars of the canal.

The water did not flow ahead; it spread itself out in the fields of Batiste, which drank and drank with the thirst of a dropsical man.

Perhaps those down below were complaining; perhaps Pimentó, notified as an *atandador*, was prowling in the vicinity, outraged at this insolent breach of the law.

But here was Batiste, like a sentinel of his harvest, a hero made desperate by the struggle of his family, guarding his people who were moving about in the field, extending the irrigation; ready to deal a blow at the first who might attempt to raise the bars, and re-establish the water's course.

So fierce was the attitude of this great fellow who stood out motionless in the midst of the canal; in this black phantom there might be divined such a resolution of shooting at whoever might present himself, that no one ventured forth from the adjoining canebrake, and the fields drank for an hour without any protest.

And this is what is yet stranger: on the following Thursday the *atandador* did not have him summoned before the Tribunal of the Waters.

The *huerta* had been informed that in the ancient farmhouse of Barret the only object of worth was a double-barreled shotgun, recently bought by the intruder, with that African passion of the Valencian, who willingly deprives himself of bread in order to have behind the door of his house a new weapon which excites envy and inspires respect.

V

EVERY morning, at dawn, Roseta, Batiste's daughter, leaped out of bed, her eyes heavy with sleep, and after stretching out her arms in graceful writhings which shook all her body of blonde slenderness, opened the farm-house door.

The pulley of the well creaked, the ugly little dog, which passed the night outside the house, leaped close to her skirts, barking with joy, and Roseta, in the light of the last stars, cast over her face and hands a pail of cold water drawn from that round and murky hole, crowned at the top by thick clumps of ivy.

Afterward, in the light of the candle, she moved about the house preparing for her journey to Valencia.

The mother followed her without seeing her from the bed with all kinds of suggestions. She could take away what was left from the supper: that with three sardines which she would find on the shelf would be sufficient. And take care

not to break the dish as she did the other day.
Ah! And she should not forget to buy thread,
needles and some sandals for the little one.
Destructive child! . . . She would find the
money in the drawer of the little table.

And while the mother turned over in bed,
sweetly caressed by the warmth of the bedroom,
planning to sleep a half-hour more close to the
enormous Batiste, who snored noisily, Roseta
continued her evolutions. She placed her poor
meal in a basket, passed a comb through her
light-blond hair, which looked as though the
sun had absorbed its colour, and tied the handkerchief under her chin. Before going out, she
looked with the tender solicitousness of an elder
sister, to see if the little ones who slept on the
floor, all in the same room, were well covered.
They lay there in a row from the eldest to the
youngest, from the overgrown Batistet to the little tot who as yet could hardly talk, like a row
of organ pipes.

"Good-bye, until tonight!" shouted the brave
girl, and passing her arm through the handle
of the basket, she closed the door of the farm-
house, placing the key underneath.

It was already daylight. In the bluish light

of dawn the procession of workers could be seen passing over the paths and roads, all walking in the same direction, drawn by the life of the city.

Groups of graceful spinning-mill girls passed by, marching with an even step, swinging with jaunty grace their right arms which cut the air like a strong oar, and all screaming in chorus every time that any strapping young fellow saluted them from the neighbouring fields with coarse jests.

Roseta walked to the city alone. Well did the poor child know her companions, daughters and sisters of those who hated her family so bitterly.

Several of them were working in the factory, and the poor little yellow-haired girl, making a show of courage more than once, had to defend herself by sheer scratching. Taking advantage of her carelessness, they threw dirty things into her lunch-basket; made her break the earthenware dish of which she was reminded so many times, and never passed near her in the mill without trying to push her over the smoking kettle where the cocoon was being soaked while they called her a pauper, and applied similar eulogies to her and her family.

On the way she fled from them as from a throng of furies, and felt safe only when she was inside the factory, an ugly old building close to the market, whose façades, painted in water-colours the century before, still preserved between peeling paint and cracks certain groups of rose-coloured legs, and profiles of bronzed colour, remnants of medallions, and mythological paintings.

Of all the family, Roseta was the most like her father: a fury for work, as Batiste said of himself. The fiery vapour of the caldron where the cocoon is soaked mounted about her head, burning her eyes; but, in spite of this, she was always in her place, fishing in the depths of the boiling water for the loosened ends of those capsules of soft silk of the mellow colour of caramel, in whose interior the laborious worm, the larva of precious exudation, had just perished for the offence of creating a rich dungeon for its transformation into the butterfly.

Throughout the large building reigned the din of work, deafening and tiresome for the daughters of the *huerta*, who were used to the calm of the immense plain, where the voice carries a great distance. Below roared the steam-engine, giving forth frightful roaring sounds which were transmitted through the multiple tubing: pulleys and wheels revolved with an infernal din, and as though there were not noise enough, the spinning-mill girls, according to traditional custom, sang in chorus with a nasal voice, the *Padre nuestro,* the *Ave Maria,* and the *Gloria Patri,* with the same musical interludes as the chorus which roamed about the *huerta* Sunday mornings at dawn.

This did not prevent them from laughing as they sang, nor from insulting each other in an undertone between prayers, and threatening each other with four long scratches on coming out, for these dark-complexioned girls, enslaved by the rigid tyranny which rules in the farmer's family, and obliged by hereditary conventions to lower their eyes in the presence of men, when gathered together without restraint were regular demons, and took delight in uttering everything they had heard from the cart-drivers and labourers on the roads.

Roseta was the most silent and industrious of them all. In order not to distract her attention from her work, she did not sing; she never provoked quarrels and she learned everything with

such facility, that in a few weeks she was earning three reals, almost the maximum for the
day's work, to the great envy of the others.

At the lunch-hour these bands of dishevelled
girls sallied forth from the factory to gobble up
the contents of their earthen-ware dishes. As
they formed a loafing group on the side-walk or
in the immediate porches, and challenged the
men with insolent glances to speak to them, only
falsely scandalized, to fire back shameless re-
marks in return, Roseta remained in a corner of
the mill, seated on the floor with two or three
good girls who were from another *huerta*, from
the right side of the river, and who did not care
a rap for the story of old Barret and the hatred
of their companions.

During the first weeks, Roseta saw with a certain terror the arrival of dusk, and with it, the
hour for departure.

Fearing her companions, who took the same
road as herself, she stayed in the factory for a
time, letting them set out ahead like a cyclone,
with scandalous bursts of laughter, flauntings of
skirts, daring vulgarisms, and the odour of
health, of hard and rugged limbs.

She walked lazily through the streets of the

city in the cold twilight of winter, making purchases for her mother, stood open-mouthed before the shop windows which began to be illumined, and at last, passing over the bridge, she
entered the dark narrow alleys of the suburbs
to set forth upon the road of Alboraya.

So far, all was well. But after she came to
the dark *huerta* with its mysterious noises, its
dark and alarming forms which passed close to
her saluting with a deep "Good night," fear set
in, and her teeth chattered.

And it was not that the silence and the darkness intimidated her. Like a true daughter of
the country, she was accustomed to these. If
she had been certain that she would encounter no
one on the road, it would have given her confidence. In her terror, she never thought, as did
her companions, of death, nor of witches and
phantasms; it was the living who disturbed her.

She recalled with growing fear certain stories
of the *huerta* that she had heard in the factory;
the fear that the little girls had of Pimentó, and
other bullies who congregated in the tavern of
Copa: heartless fellows who pinched the girls
wherever they could, and pushed them into the
canals, or made them fall behind the haylofts.

And Roseta, who was no longer innocent after entering the factory, gave free rein to her imagination, till it reached the utmost limits of the horrible; and she saw herself assassinated by some one of these monsters, her stomach ripped up and soaked in blood, like those children of the legends of the *huerta* whose fat sinister and mysterious murderers extracted and used in making wonderful salves and potions for the rich.

In the twilight of winter, dark and oftentimes rainy, Roseta passed over more than half of the road all a tremble. But the most cruel crisis, the most terrible obstacle was almost at the end, and close to the farm—the famous tavern of Copa.

Here was the den of the wild beast. This was the most frequented and the brightest bit of road. The sound of voices, the outbursts of laughter, the thrumming of a guitar, and couplets of songs with loud shouting came forth from the door which, like the mouth of a furnace, cast forth a square of reddish light over the black road, in which grotesque shadows moved about. And nevertheless, the poor mill girl, on arriving near this place, stopped undecided, trembling like the heroines of the fairy-tales before the den of the

ogre, ready to set out through the fields in order
to make a détour around the rear of the building,
to sink into the canal which bordered the road,
and to slip away hidden behind the sloping
banks; anything rather than to pass in front of
this red gullet which gave forth the din of drunkenness and brutality.

Finally she decided; made an effort of will
like one who is going to throw himself over a
high cliff, and passed swiftly before the tavern,
along the edge of the canal, with a very light
step, and the marvellous poise which fear
lends.

She was a breath, a white shadow which did
not give the turbid eyes of the customers of Copa
time to fix themselves upon it.

And the tavern passed, the child ran and ran,
believing that some one was just behind her, expecting to feel the tug of his powerful paw at
her skirt.

She was not calm until she heard the barking
of the dog at the farmhouse, that ugly animal,
who by way of antithesis no doubt, was called
The Morning Star, and who came bounding up
to her in the middle of the road with bounds and
licked her hands.

Roseta never told those at home of the terrors encountered on the road. The poor child composed herself on entering the house, and answered the questions of her anxious mother quietly, meeting the situation valorously by stating that she had come home with some companions.

The spinning-mill girl did not want her father to come out nights to accompany her on the road. She knew the hatred of the neighbourhood: the tavern of Copa with its quarrelsome people inspired her with fear.

And on the following day she returned to the factory to suffer the same fears upon returning, enlivened only by the hope that the spring would soon come with its longer days and its luminous twilights, which would permit her to return to the house before it grew dark.

One night, Roseta experienced a certain relief. While she was still close to the city, a man came out upon the road and began to walk at the same pace as herself.

"Good evening!"

And while the mill-girl was walking over the high bank which bordered the read, the man walked below, among the deep cuts opened by

the wheels of the carts, stumbling over the red
bricks, chipped dishes, and even pieces of glass
with which farsighted hands wished to fill up the
holes of remote origin.

Roseta showed no disquietude. She had
recognized her companion even before he saluted her. It was Tonet, the nephew of old
Tomba, the shepherd: a good boy, who served as
an apprentice to a butcher of Alboraya, and at
whom the mill-girls laughed when they met him
upon the road, taking delight in seeing how he
blushed, and turned his head away at the least
word.

Such a timid boy! He was alone in the world
without any other relatives than his grandfather,
worked even on Sundays, and not only went to
Valencia to collect manure for the fields of his
master, but also helped him in the slaughter of
cattle and tilled the earth, and carried meat to the
rich farmers. All in order that he and his grandfather might eat, and that he might go dressed in
the old ragged clothes of his master. He did
not smoke; he had entered the tavern of Copa
only two or three times in his life, and on Sundays, if he had some hours free, instead of squatting on the Plaza of Alboraya, like the others to

watch the bullies playing hand-ball, he went out
into the fields and roamed aimlessly through the
tangled net-work of paths.   If he happened to
meet a tree filled with birds, he would stop there
fascinated by the fluttering and the cries of these
vagrants of the air.

The people saw in him something of the mysterious eccentricities of his grandfather, the
shepherd: all regarded him as a poor fool, timid
and docile.

The mill-girl became enlivened with company.
She was safer if a man walked with her, and
more so if it were Tonet, who inspired confidence.

She spoke to him, asking him whence he came,
and the youth answered vaguely, with his habitual timidity: "From there . . . from there.
. . ." and then became silent as if those words
cost him a great effort.

They followed the road in silence, parting
close to the *barraca.*

"Good night and thanks!" said the girl.

"Good night," and Tonet disappeared, walking toward the village.

It was an incident of no importance, an agreeable encounter which had banished her fear,
nothing more.   And nevertheless, Roseta ate

supper that night and went to bed thinking of old Tomba's nephew.

Now she recalled the times that she had met him mornings on the road, and it seemed to her that Tonet always tried to keep the same pace as herself, although somewhat apart so as not to attract the attention of the sarcastic mill-girls. It even seemed to her that at times, on turning her head suddenly, she had surprised him with his eyes fixed upon her.

And the girl, as if she were spinning a cocoon, grasped these loose ends of her memory, and drew and drew them out, recalling everything in her existence which related to Tonet: the first time that she saw him, and her impulse of sympathetic compassion on account of the mockery of the mill-girls which he suffered crestfallen and timid, as though these harpies in a troop inspired him with fear; then the frequent encounters on the road, and the fixed glances of the boy, who seemed to wish to say something to her.

The following day, when she went to Valencia, she did not see him, but at night, upon starting to return to the *barraca*, the girl was not afraid in spite of the twilight being dark and rainy.

She foresaw that the companion who gave her such courage would put in an appearance, and true enough he came out to meet her at almost the same spot as on the preceding day.

He was as expressive as usual: "Good night!" and went on walking at her side.

Roseta was more loquacious. Where did he come from? What a chance to meet on two succeeding days! And he, trembling, as though the words cost him a great effort, answered as usual: "From there . . . from there . . ."

The girl, just as timid, felt nevertheless a temptation to laugh at his agitation. She spoke of her fear, and the scares which she had met with on the road during the winter, and Tonet, comforted by the service which he was lending to her, unglued his lips at last, in order to tell her that he would accompany her frequently. He always had business for his master in the *huerta*.

They took leave of each other with the brevity of the preceding day; but that night the girl went to her bed restless and nervous, and dreamed a thousand wild things; she saw herself on a black road, very black, accompanied by an enormous dog which licked her hands and had the same

face as Tonet; and afterward there came a wolf
to bite her, with a snout which vaguely reminded
her of the hateful Pimentó; and the two fought
with their teeth, and her father came out with a
club, and she was weeping as if the blows which
her faithful dog received were falling on her own
shoulders; and thus her imagination went on wandering. But in all the confused scenes of her
dream she saw the grandson of old Tomba, with
his blue eyes, and his boyish face covered with
light down, first indication of his manhood.

She arose weak and broken as if she were coming out of a delirium. This was Sunday, and
she was not going to the factory. The sun came
in through the little window of her bedroom, and
all the people of the farmhouse were already out
of their beds. Roseta began to get ready to go
with her mother to church.

The diabolical dream still upset her. She
felt differently, with different thoughts, as though
the preceding night were a wall which divided
her existence into two parts.

She sang gaily like a bird while she took her
clothes out of the chest, and arranged them upon
the bed, which, still warm, held the impress of
her body.

She liked these Sundays with her freedom
to arise late, with her hours of leisure, and her
little trip to Alboraya to hear mass; but this
Sunday was better than the others; the sun shone
more brightly, the birds were singing with more
passion, through the little window the air entered
gloriously balsamic; how should one express it!
in short, this morning had something new and
extraordinary about it.

She reproached herself now for having up to
that time paid no attention to her personal appearance. It is time, at sixteen, to think about
fixing oneself up. How stupid she had been, always laughing at her mother who called her a
dowdy! And as though it were new attire which
she looked on for the first time, she drew
over her head as carefully as if it were thin lace,
the calico petticoat which she wore every Sunday; and laced her corset tightly, as though that
armour of high whalebones, a real farmer-girl's
corset, which crushed the budding breasts
cruelly, were not already tight enough. For in
the *huerta* it is considered immodest for unmarried girls not to hide the alluring charms of nature, so that no one might sinfully behold in the
virgin the symbols of her future maternity.

For the first time in her life, the mill-girl
passed more than a quarter of an hour before
the four inches of looking-glass, in its frame of
varnished pine, which her father had presented
to her, a mirror in which she had to look at her
face by sections.

She was not beautiful, and she knew it; but
uglier ones she had met by the dozen in the
huerta. And without knowing why, she took
pleasure in contemplating her eyes, of a clear
green; the cheeks spotted with delicate freckles
which the sun had raised upon the tanned skin;
the whitish blond hair, which had the wan
delicacy of silk; the little nose with its palpitat-
ing nostrils, projecting over the mouth; the
mouth itself, shadowed by soft down, tender as
that on a ripe peach, her strong and even teeth,
of the flashing whiteness of milk, and a gleam
which seemed to light up the whole face: the teeth
of a poor girl!

The mother had to wait; the poor woman was
in a hurry, moving about the house impatiently
as though spurred on by the bell which sounded
from a distance. They were going to miss mass:
and meanwhile Roseta was calmly combing her
hair, constantly undoing her work, which did

not satisfy her; she went on arranging the mantle
with tugs of vexation, never finding it to her
liking.

In the *plaza* of Alboraya, upon entering and
leaving the church, Roseta, hardly raising her
eyes, scanned the door of the meat-market, where
the people were crowding in, coming from mass.

There he was, assisting his master, giving him
the flayed pieces of meat, and driving away the
swarms of flies which were covering it.

How the big simpleton flushed on seeing
her.

As she passed the second time, he remained
like one who has been charmed, with a leg of
mutton in his hand, while his stout employer,
waiting in vain for him to pass it to him, poured
forth a round volley of oaths, threatening the
youth with a cleaver.

She was sad that afternoon. Seated at the
door of the farmhouse, she believed she saw him
several times prowling about the distant paths,
and hiding in the cane-brake to watch her. The
mill-girl wished that Monday might arrive soon,
so she might go back to the factory, and come
home over the horrible road accompanied by
Tonet.

The boy did not fail her at dusk on the following day.

Even nearer to the city than upon the other
nights, he came forth to meet her.

"Good evening!"

But after the customary salutation, he was not
silent.   The rogue had made progress on the day
of rest.

And slowly, accompanying his expressions
with grimaces, and scratches upon his trousers-
legs, he tried to explain himself, although at
times a full two minutes passed between his
words.   He was happy at seeing her well.   (A
smile from Roseta and a "thanks," murmured
faintly.)   "Had she enjoyed herself Sunday?"
. . . (Silence.)   "He had had quite a dull time.
It had bored him.   Doubtless, the custom . . .
then . . . it seemed that something had been
lacking . . . naturally he had taken a fancy for
the road . . . no, not the road: what he liked
was to accompany her. . . ."

And here he stopped high and dry: it even
seemed to him that he bit his tongue nervously
to punish it for its boldness and pinched himself
for having gone so far.

They walked some distance in silence. The
girl did not answer; she went along her way with
the gracefully affected air of the mill-girls, the
basket at the left hip, and the right arm cutting
the air with the swinging motion of a pendulum.

She was thinking of her dream; she imagined
herself again to be in the midst of that delirium, seeing wild phantasies; several times she
turned her head, believing that she saw in the
twilight the dog which had licked her hands,
and which had the face of Tonet, a remembrance
which even made her laugh. But no; he who
was at her side was a good fellow capable of defending her; somewhat timid and bashful, yes,
with his head drooping, as though it hurt him to
bring forth the words which he had just spoken.

Roseta even confused him the more. Come
now; why did he go out to meet her on the way?
What would the people say? If her father
should be informed, how annoyed he would be!

"Why? Why?" asked the girl.

And the youth, sadder and sadder, and more
and more timid, like a convicted culprit who
hears his accusation, answered nothing. He
walked along at the same pace as the girl, but

apart from her, stumbling along the edge of the road.   Roseta almost believed that he was going to cry.

But when they were near the *barraca,* and as they were about to separate, Tonet had an impulse: as he had been intensely silent, so now he was intensely eloquent, and as though many minutes had not elapsed, he answered the question of the girl:

"Why? . . . because I love you."

As he said it he approached her so closely that she even felt his breath on her face and his eyes glowed as if through them all the truth must go out to her; and after this, repenting again, afraid, terrified by his words, he began to run like a child.

So then he loved her! . . . For two days the girl had been expecting the word, and nevertheless, it gave her the effect of a sudden, unexpected revelation.   She also loved him, and all that night, even in dreams, she heard him murmuring a thousand times, close to her ears, the same words:

"Because I love you."

Tonet did not await her the following night. At dawn Roseta saw him on the road, almost hidden behind the trunk of a mulberry-tree, watching her with anxiety, like a child who fears a reprimand and has repented, ready to flee at the first gesture of displeasure.

But the mill-girl smiled blushingly, and there was need of nothing more.

All was said: they did not tell each other again that they loved each other, but this matter decided their betrothal, and Tonet no longer failed a single time to accompany her on the road.

The stout butcher of Alboraya blustered with anger at the sudden change in his servant, so far so diligent, and now ever inventing pretexts to pass hours and ever more hours in the *huerta*, especially at night.

But with the selfishness of happiness, Tonet cared no more for the oaths and threats of his master than the mill-girl did for her father, for whom she felt more fear than respect.

Roseta always had some nest or other in her bedroom, which she claimed to have found upon the road. This boy did not know how to present himself with empty hands, and explored all the cane-brake and the trees of the *huerta* in order to present her, his betrothed, with round mats of straw and twigs, in whose depths were some little rogues of fledgelings whose rosy skin was covered with the finest down, peeping desperately as they opened their monstrous beaks, always hungry for more crumbs of bread.

Roseta guarded the gift in her room, as though it were the very person of her betrothed, and wept when her brothers, the little people who had the farmhouse for a nest, showed their admiration for the birds so strenuously that they ended by stifling them.

At other times, Tonet appeared with his clothes bulging, his sash filled with lupines and peanuts bought in the tavern of Copa, and as they walked along the road, they would eat and eat, gazing into each other's eyes, smiling like fools, without knowing why, often seating themselves upon a bank, without realizing it.

She was the more sensible and scolded him. Always spending money! There were two reals or a little less, which, in a week's time, he had left at the tavern for such treats. And he showed himself to be generous. For whom did he want the money if not for her? When they would be married—which had to happen some day—he would then take care of his money. That, however, would not be for ten or twelve years; there was no need of haste; all the betrothals of the *huerta* lasted for some time.

The matter of the wedding brought Roseta back to reality. The day her father would learn of it. . . . Most holy Virgin! he would break her back with a club. And she spoke of the future thrashing with serenity, smiling like a strong girl accustomed to this parental authority, rigid, imposing, and respected, which manifested itself in cuffs and cudgels.

Their relations were innocent. Never did there arise between them the poignant and rebellious desire of the flesh. They walked along the almost deserted road in the dusk of the evening-fall, and solitude seemed to drive all impure thoughts from their minds.

Once when Tonet involuntarily and lightly touched Roseta's waist, he blushed as if he, not she, were the girl in question.

They were both very far from thinking that their daily meeting might result in something more than words and glances. It was the first love, the budding of scarcely awakened youth, content with seeing, speaking, laughing, without a trace of sensual desire.

The mill-girl, who on the nights of fear, had

longed so for the coming of spring, saw with anxiety the arrival of the long and luminous twilights.

Now she met her betrothed in full daylight,
and there were never lacking companions of
the factory or some neighbour along the road,
who on seeing them together smiled maliciously,
guessing the truth.

In the factory, jokes were started by all her
enemies, who asked her with sarcasm when the
wedding was to take place and nicknamed her
The Shepherdess, for being in love with the
grandson of old Tomba.

Poor Roseta trembled with anxiety. What a
thrashing she was going to bring upon herself!
Any day the news might reach her father's ears.
And then it was that Batiste, on the day of his
sentence in the Tribunal of the Waters, saw her
on the road, accompanied by Tonet.

But nothing happened. The happy incident
of the irrigation saved her. Her father, contented at having saved the crops, limited himself
to looking at her several times, with his eyebrows
puckered, and to notifying her in a slow voice,
forefinger raised in air, and with an imperative
accent, that henceforth she should take care to

return alone from the factory, or otherwise she would learn who he was.

And she came back alone during all the week. Tonet had a certain respect for Señor Batiste, and contented himself with hiding in the cane-brake, near the road, to watch the mill-girl pass by, or to follow her from a distance.

As the days now were longer, there were more people on the road.

But this separation could not be prolonged for the impatient lovers, and one Sunday afternoon, Roseta, inactive, tired of walking in front of the door of her house, and believing she saw Tonet in all who were passing over the neighbouring paths, seized a green-varnished pitcher, and told her mother that she was going to bring water from the fountain of the Queen.

The mother allowed her to go. She ought to divert herself; poor girl! she did not have any friends and you must let youth claim its own.

The fountain of the Queen was the pride of all that part of the *huerta*, condemned to the water of the wells and the red and muddy liquid which ran through the canals.

It was in front of an abandoned farmhouse, and was old and of great merit, according to the wisest of the *huerta;* the work of the Moors, according to Pimentó; a monument of the epoch when the apostles were baptizing sinners as they went about the world, so that oracle, old Tomba, declared with majesty.

In the afternoons, passing along the road, bordered by poplars with their restless foliage of silver, one might see groups of girls with their pitchers held motionless and erect upon their heads, reminding one with their rhythmical step and their slender figures of the Greek basket-bearers.

This defile gave to the Valencian *huerta* something of a Biblical flavour; it recalled Arabic poetry, which sings of the woman beside the fountain with the pitcher on her head, uniting in the same picture the two most vehement passions of the Oriental: beauty and water.

The fountain of the Queen was a four-sided pool, with walls of red stone, and the water below at the level of the ground. One descended by a half-dozen steps, always slippery and green with humidity. On the surface of the rectangle of stone facing the stairs a bas-relief projected, but the figures were indistinct; it was impossible to make them out beneath the coat of whitewash.

It was probably the Virgin surrounded by angels; a work of the rough and simple art of the
Middle Ages; some votive offering of the time
of the conquest: but with some generations pick-
ing at the stones, in order to mark better the
figures obliterated by the years, and others white-
washing them with the sudden impulse of barbaric curiosity, had left the slab in such condition that nothing except the shapeless form of a
woman could be distinguished, the queen who
gave her name to the fountain: the queen of the
Moors, as all queens necessarily must be in all
country-tales.

Nor was the shouting and the confusion a
small matter here on Sunday afternoons. More
than thirty girls would crowd together with their
pitchers, desiring to be the first to fill them, but
then in no hurry to go away. They pushed each
other on the narrow stairway, with their skirts
tucked in between their limbs, in order to bend
over and sink the pitcher into the pool, whose
surface trembled with the bubbles of water which
incessantly surged up from the bottom of the
sand, where clumps of gelatinous plants were
growing, green tufts of hair-like fibres, waving in
the prison of crystal liquid, trembling with the

impulse of the current.   The restless water-skip-
pers streaked across the clear surface with their
delicate legs.

Those who had already filled their pitchers sat
down on the edge of the pool, hanging their legs
over the water and drawing them in with scandalized screams whenever a boy came down to drink
and looked up at them.

It was a reunion of turbulent gamin.   All
were talking at the same time; they insulted each
other, they flayed those who were absent, revealing all the scandal of the *huerta,* and the young
people, free from parental severity, cast off the
hypocritical expression assumed for the house,
revealing an aggressiveness characteristic of
the uncultured who lack expansion.   These an-
gelic brunettes, who sang songs to the Virgin and
litanies in the church of Alboraya so softly when
the festival of the unmarried women was celebrated, now on being alone, became bold and
enlivened their conversation with the curses of a
teamster, speaking of secret things with the calm-
ness of old women.

Roseta arrived here with her pitcher, without
having met her betrothed upon the road, in spite
of the fact that she had walked slowly and had

turning her head frequently, hoping at every moment to see him come forth from a path.

The noisy party at the fountain became silent on seeing her. The presence of Roseta at first caused stupefaction: somewhat like the apparition of a Moor in the church of Alboraya in the midst of high mass. Why did this pauper come here?

Roseta greeted two or three who were from the factory, but they pinched their lips with an expression of scorn and hardly answered her.

The others, recovered from their surprise, and not wishing to concede to the intruder even the honour of silence, went on talking as though nothing had happened.

Roseta descended to the fountain, filled the pitcher and stood up, casting anxious glances above the wall, around over all the plain.

"Look away, look away, but he won't come! "

It was a niece of Pimentó who said this; the daughter of a sister of Pepeta, a dark, nervous girl, with an upturned and insolent nose, proud of being an only daughter, and of the fact that her father was nobody's tenant, as the four fields which he was working were his own.

Yes; she might go on looking as much as she

pleased, but he would not come. Didn't the
others know whom she was expecting? Her betrothed, the nephew of old Tomba: a fine ar-
rangement!

And the thirty cruel mouths laughed and
laughed as though every laugh were a bite; not
because they considered it a great joke, but in
order to crush the daughter of the hated Batiste.

The shepherdess! . . . The divine shepherdess!

Roseta shrugged her shoulders with indifference. She was expecting this: moreover, the
jokes of the factory had blunted her suscepti-
bility.

She took the pitcher and went down the steps,
but at the bottom the little mimicking voice of the
niece of Pimentó held her. How that small in-
sect could sting!

"She would not marry the grandson of old
Tomba. He was a poor fool, dying of hunger,
but very honourable and incapable of becoming
related to a family of thieves."

Roseta almost dropped her pitcher. She grew
red as if the words, tearing at her heart, had

made all the blood rise to her face; then she became deathly pale.

"Who is a thief? Who?" she asked with trembling voice, which made all the others at the fountain laugh.

Who? Her father. Pimentó, her uncle, knew it well, and in the tavern of Copa nothing else was discussed. Did they believe that the past could be hidden? They had fled from their own *pueblo* because they were known there too well: for that reason they had come here, to take possession of what was not theirs. They had even heard that Señor Batiste had been in prison for ugly crimes.

And thus the little viper went on talking, pouring forth everything that she had heard in her house and in the *huerta:* the lies forged by the dissolute fellows at the tavern of Copa, all invented by Pimentó, who was growing less and less disposed to attack Batiste face to face, and way trying to annoy him, to persecute and wound him with insults.

The determination of the father suddenly surged up in Roseta. Trembling, stammering with fury, and with bloodshot eyes, she dropped

the pitcher, which broke into pieces drenching
the nearest girls, who protested in a chorus, calling her a stupid creature. But she was in no
mood to take notice of such things!

"My father . . ." she cried, advancing toward the one who had insulted her. "My father
a thief? Say that again and I will smash your
face!"

But the dark-haired girl did not have to repeat
it, for before she could open her lips, she received a blow in the mouth, and the fingers of
Roseta fixed themselves in her hair. Instinctively, impelled by pain, she seized the blond
hair of the mill-girl in turn, and for some time
the two could be seen struggling together, bent
over, pouring forth cries of pain and madness,
with their foreheads almost touching the ground,
dragged this way and that by the cruel tugs which
each one gave to the head of the other. The
hair-pins fell out, loosening the braids; the heavy
heads of hair seemed like banners of war, not
floating and victorious, but crumpled and torn
by the hands of the opponent.

But Roseta, either stronger or more furious,
succeeded in disengaging herself, and was going
to drag her enemy to her, perhaps to give her a

spanking, for she was trying to take off her slip-
per with her free hand, when there occurred an
irritating, brutal, unheard-of scene.

Without any spoken agreement, as if all the
hatred of their families, all the words and maledictions heard in their homes, had surged up in
them at a bound, all threw themselves together
upon the daughter of Batiste.

"Thief!   Thief!"

In the twinkling of an eye, Roseta disappeared
under the wrathful arms.   Her face was covered
with scratches; she was carried down by the
shower of blows, though unable to fall, for the
very crush of her enemies impeded her; but
driven from one side to the other, she ended by
rolling down head-long on the slippery stones,
striking her forehead on an angle of the stone.

Blood!   It was like the casting of a stone into
a tree covered with sparrows.   They flew away,
all of them, running in different directions, with
their pitchers on their heads, and in a short time
no one could be seen in the vicinity of the fountain of the Queen but poor Roseta, who with loosened hair, skirts torn, face dirty with dust and
blood, went crying home.

How her mother screamed when she saw her

come in! How she protested upon being told of
what had occurred! Those people were worse
than Jews! Lord! Lord! Could such crimes
occur in a land of Christians?

It was impossible to live. They had not done
enough already with the men attacking poor Batiste, persecuting him and slandering him before
the Tribunal, and imposing unjust fines upon
him. Now here were these girls persecuting her
poor Roseta, as though that unfortunate child had
done anything wrong. And why was it all?
Because they wished to earn a living and work,
without offending anybody, as God commanded.

Batiste turned pale as he looked at his daughter. He took a few steps toward the road, looking at Pimentó's farmhouse, whose roof stood
out behind the canes.

But he stopped and finally began to reproach
his daughter mildly. What had occurred would
teach her not to go walking about the *huerta*.
They must avoid all contact with others: live together and united in the farmhouse and never
leave these lands which were their life.

His enemies would take good care not to seek
him out in his own home.

VI

A WASP-LIKE buzzing, the murmur of a bee-hive, was what the dwellers in the *huerta* heard as they passed before the Cadena mill by the road leading to the sea.

A thick curtain of poplar-trees closed in the little square formed by the road as it widened before the heap of old tiled roofs, cracked walls and small black windows of the mill, the latter an old and tumble-down structure erected over the canal and based on thick buttresses, between which poured the water's foaming cascade.

The slow, monotonous noise that seemed to issue from between the trees came from Don Joaquín's school, situated in a farm-house hidden by the row of poplar-trees.

Never was knowledge worse-lodged, though wisdom does not often, to be sure, dwell in palaces.

An old farm-house, with no other light than from the door and that which filtered in through

155

the cracks of the roofs: the walls of doubtful
whiteness, for the master's wife, a stout lady who
lived in her rush-chair, passed the day listening
to her husband and admiring him; a few benches,
three grimy alphabets, torn at the ends, fastened
to the wall with bits of chewed bread, and in the
room adjoining the school some few old pieces
of furniture which seemed to have knocked about
half of Spain.

In the whole *barraca* there was one new object: the long cane which the master kept behind
the door and which he renewed every couple of
days from the nearby cane-brake; it was very
fortunate that the material was so cheap, for it
was rapidly used up on the hard, close-clipped
heads of those small savages.

Only three books could be seen in the school;
the same primer served for all. Why should
there be more? There reigned the Moorish
method; sing-song and repetition, till with con-
tinual pounding you got things into their hard
heads.

Hence from morning to night the old farm-
house sent from its door a wearisome sing-song
which all the birds of the neighbourhood made
fun of.

"Our . . . fa . . . ther, who . . . art . . . in heaven."

"Holy . . . Mary . . ."

"Two times two . . . fo . . . up . . ."

And the sparrows, the linnets, and the calendar larks who fled from the youngsters when they saw them in a band on the roads, alighted with the greatest confidence on the nearest trees, and even hopped up and down with their springy little feet before the door of the school, laughing scandalously at their fierce enemies on seeing them thus caged up, under the threat of the rattan, condemned to gaze at them sideways, without moving, and repeating the same wearisome and unlovely song.

From time to time the chorus stilled and the voice of Don Joaquín rose majestically, pouring out his fund of knowledge in a stream.

"How many works of mercy are there?"

"Two times seven are how many?"

And rarely was he satisfied with the answers.

"You are a lot of dunces. You sit there listening as though I were talking Greek. And to think that I treat you with all courtesy, as in a city college, so you may learn good forms and know how to talk like persons of breeding! . . .

In short, you have some one to imitate. But you are as rough and ignorant as your parents, who are also dishonest: they have money left to go to the tavern and they invent a thousand excuses to avoid giving me Saturdays the two coppers that are due me."

And he walked up and down indignant as he always was when he complained of the Saturday omissions. You could see it in his hair and in his figure, which seemed to be divided into two parts.

Below, his torn hempen-sandals always stained with mud: his old cloth trousers; his rough, scaly hands, which retained in the fissures of the skin the dirt of his little orchard, a square of garden-truck which he owned in front of the school-house, and many times this produce was all that went into his stew.

But from the waist upward his nobility was shown, "the dignity of the priest of knowledge," as he would say; that which distinguished him from all the population of the farm-houses, worms fastened to the glebe; a necktie of loud colours over his dirty shirt-front, a grey and bristly moustache, cutting his chubby and ruddy face, and a blue cap with an oilcloth visor, sou-

venir of one of the many positions he had filled
in his chequered career.

This was what consoled him for his poverty;
especially the necktie, which no one else in the
whole district wore, and which he exhibited as a
sign of supreme distinction, a species of golden
fleece, as it were, of the *huerta*.

The people of the farm-houses respected Don
Joaquín, though as regards the assistance of his
poverty they were remiss and slothful. What
that man had seen! How he had travelled over
the world! Several times a railway employé;
other times helping to collect taxes in the most
remote provinces of Spain; it was even said that
he had been a policeman in America. In short,
he was a "somebody" in reduced circumstances.

"Don Joaquín," his stout wife would say,
who was always the first to give him his title,
"has never seen himself in the position he is in
today; we are of a good family. Misfortune
has brought us to this, but in our time we have
made a mint of money."

And the gossips of the *huerta*, despite the fact
that they sometimes forgot to send the two coppers for the instruction Saturdays, respected Don
Joaquín as a superior being, reserving the right

to make a little sport of his short jacket, which was green and had square tails; and which he wore on holidays, when he sang at high mass in the choir of Alboraya church.

Driven by poverty, he had landed there with his obese and flabby better-half as he might have landed anywhere else. He helped the secretary of the village with extra work; he prepared with herbs known only to himself certain brews which accomplished wonders in the farmhouses, where they all admitted that that old chap knew a lot; and without the title of schoolmaster, but with no fear that any one else would try to take away from him a school which did not bring in enough even to buy bread, he succeeded by much repetition and many canings, in teaching all the urchins of five or ten, who on holidays threw stones at the birds, stole fruit, and chased the dogs on the roads of the *huerta*, to spell and to keep quiet.

Where had the master come from? All the wives of the neighbours knew, from beyond the *churrería*. And vainly were further explanations asked, for as far as the geography of the *huerta* was concerned, all those who do not speak Valencian are of the *churrería*.

Don Joaquín had no small difficulty in making his pupils understand him and preventing them from being afraid of Castilian. There were some who had been two months in school and who opened their eyes wide and scratched the backs of their heads without understanding what the master who used words never heard before in his school said to them.

How the good man suffered! He who attributed all the triumphs of his teaching to his refinement, to his distinction of manners, to his use of good language, as his wife declared!

Every word which his pupils pronounced badly (and they did not pronounce one well), made him groan and raise his hands indignantly till they touched the smoky ceiling of his schoolhouse. Nevertheless he was proud of the urbanity with which he treated his pupils.

"You should look upon this humble schoolhouse," he would say to the twenty youngsters who crowded and pushed one another on the narrow benches, listening to him half-bored and half-afraid of his rattan, "as a temple of courtesy and good-breeding. Temple, did I say? It is the torch that shines and dissolves the barbaric darkness of this *huerta*. Without me, what

would you be? Beasts, and pardon me the
word; the same as your worthy fathers whom I
do not wish to offend! But with God's aid you
must leave here educated, able to present your-
selves anywhere, since you have had the good
fortune to find a master like me. Isn't that so?"

And the boys replied with furious noddings,
some knocking their heads against their neighbours' heads; and even his wife, moved by the
temple and the torch, stopped knitting her stocking and pushed back the rush-chair to envelop her
husband in a glance of admiration.

He would question all the band of dirty urchins whose feet were bare and whose shirt-tails
were in the air, with astonishing courtesy:

"Let's see, Señor de Lopis; rise."

And Señor de Lopis, a mucker of seven with
short knee trousers held up by one suspender,
tumbled off his bench and stood at attention before the master, gazing askance at the terrible
cane.

"For some time, I 've been watching you pick-
ing your nose and making little balls of it. An
ugly habit, Señor de Lopis. Believe your master. I will let it pass this time because you are
industrious and know your multiplication table;

but knowledge is nothing when good-breeding is lacking; don't forget that, Señor de Lopis."

And the boy who made the little balls agreed with everything, overjoyed to get off without a caning. But another big boy who sat beside him on the bench and who must have been nourishing some old grudge, seeing him standing, gave him a treacherous pinch.

"Oh, oh, master!" cried the boy. "'*Orseface*' pinched me!"

What was not Don Joaquín's indignation? What most excited his anger was the fondness the boys had for calling each other by their father's nicknames and even for inventing new ones.

"Who is '*Orse*-Face'? Señor de Peris, you probably mean. What mode of address is that, great heavens! One would think you were in a drinking-house! If at least you had said *Horse*-Face! Wear yourself out teaching such idiots! Brutes!"

And raising his cane, he began to distribute resounding blows to each; to the one for the pinch and to the other for the "impropriety of language," as Don Joaquín expressed it, without stopping his whacks. And his blows were so blind that the other boys on the benches shrank together, each one hiding his head on his neighbour's shoulder; and one little fellow, the younger son of Batiste, frightened by the noise of the cane, had a movement of the bowels.

This appeased the master, made him recover his lost majesty, while the well-thrashed audience picked their noses.

"Doña Pepa," he said to his wife, "take Señor de Borrull away, for he is ill, and clean him after school."

And the old woman, who had a certain consideration for the three sons of Batiste, because they paid her husband every Saturday, seized the hand of *Señor de Borrull,* who left the school walking unsteadily on his weak little legs, still weeping with fear, and showing somewhat more than his shirttail through the rear-opening of his trousers.

These incidents concluded, the lesson-chanting was continued, and the grove trembled with displeasure, its monotonous whisper filtering through the foliage.

Sometimes a melancholy sound of bells was heard and the whole school was filled with joy. It was the flock of old Tomba approaching; all knew that when the old man arrived with his flock, there were always a couple of hours of freedom.

If the shepherd was talkative, the master was no whit behind him; both launched out on an interminable conversation, while the pupils left the benches and came close to listen, or slipping quietly away, went to play with the sheep who were grazing on the grass of the nearby slopes.

Don Joaquín liked the old man. He had seen the world, showed him the respect of speaking to him in Castilian, had a knowledge of medicinal herbs, and yet did not take from him his own customers; in short, he was the only person in the *huerta* worthy of enjoying friendly relations with him.

His appearance was always attended by the same circumstances. First the sheep arrived at the school-door, stuck their heads in, sniffed curiously and withdrew with a certain contempt, convinced that there was no food here other than intellectual, and that of small value; afterwards old Tomba appeared walking along confidently in this well-known region, holding his shepherd's crook, the only aid of his failing sight, in front of him.

He would sit down on the brick bench next to the master's door, and there the master and the shepherd would talk, silently admired by Doña Josefa and the bigger boys of the school, who would approach slowly and form a group around them.

Old Tomba, who would even talk with his sheep along the roads, spoke slowly at first like a man who fears to reveal his limitations, but the chat of the master would give him courage and soon he would plunge into the vast sea of his eternal stories. He would lament over the bad state of Spain, over what those who came from Valencia said in the *huerta*, over bad governments in general which are to blame for bad harvests, and he always would end by repeating the same thing:

"Those times, Don Joaquín, those times of mine were different. You did not know them, but your own were better than these. It's getting worse and worse. Just think what all these youngsters will see when they are men!"

This was always the introduction of his story.

"If you had only seen the followers of the Fliar!" (The shepherd could never say friar.) *"They* were true Spaniards; now there are only boasters in Copa's tavern. I was eighteen years old; I had a helmet with a copper eagle which I took from a dead man, and a gun bigger than myself. And the Fliar! . . . What a man! They talk now of General So-and-So. Lies, all lies! Where Father Nevot was, there was no one else! You should have seen him with his cassock tucked up, on his nag, with his curved sabre and pistols! How we galloped! Sometimes here, sometimes in Alicante-province, then near Albacete: they were always at our heels; but we made mince-meat of every Frenchman we caught. It seems to me I can see them still: *musiu* . . . mercy! and I, slash, slash, and a clean bayonet-thrust!"

And the wrinkled old man grew bolder and rose; his dim eyes shone like dull embers and he brandished his shepherd's staff as though he were still piercing the enemy with his bayonet. Then came the advice; behind the kind old fellow there arose a man all fierceness, with a hard, relentless heart, the product of a war to the death. His fierce instincts appeared, instincts which had, as it were, become petrified in his youth, and thus made impervious to the flight of time. He addressed the boys in Valencian, sharing with them the fruit of his experience. They must believe what he told them, for he had seen much. In life, patience to take revenge upon the enemy; to wait for the ball, and when it comes, to hit it hard. And as he gave these counsels, he winked his eyes, which in the hollows of the deep sockets seemed like dying stars on the point of flickering out. He related with senile malice a past of struggles in the *huerta,* a past of ambuscades and stratagems, and of complete contempt for the life of one's fellow-beings.

The master, fearing the moral effect of this on his pupils, would divert the course of the conversation, speaking of France, which was old Tomba's greatest memory.

It was an hour-long topic. He knew that country as well as though he had been born there. When Valencia surrendered to Marshal Suchet, he had been taken prisoner with several thousand more to a great city—Toulouse. And he intermingled in the conversation the horribly mutilated French words which he still remembered after so many years. What a country! There men went about with white plush hats, coloured coats with collars reaching up to the back of their heads, high boots like riding-boots;

and the women with skirts like flute-sheaths, so narrow that they showed all they encased; and so he went on talking of the costumes and customs of the time of the Empire, imagining that it all still continued and that France of today was as it was at the beginning of the century.

And while he related in detail all his recollections, the master and his wife listened attentively, and some of the boys, profiting by the unexpected recess, slipped away from the schoolhouse, attracted by the sheep, who fled from them as from the devil in person. For they pulled their tails and grabbed them by the legs, forcing them to walk on their fore-feet, and they sent them rolling down the slopes or tried to mount on their dirty fleece; the poor creatures protested with gentle bleatings in vain, for the shepherd did not hear them, absorbed as he was in telling with great relish of the agony of the last Frenchman who had died.

"And how many fell?" the master would ask at the end of the story.

"A matter of a hundred and twenty or thirty. I don't remember exactly."

And the husband and wife would exchange a smile. Since the last time the total had risen by

twenty.   As the years passed, his deeds of prowess and the number of victims increased.

The lamentations of the flock would attract the
master's attention.

"Gentlemen," he would call out to the rash
youths as he reached for his rattan, "come here,
all of you.   Do you imagine you can spend the
day enjoying yourself?   This is the place for
work."

And to demonstrate this by example, he would
brandish his cane so that it was a delight to see
it driving back all the flock of playful youngsters
into the sheep-fold of knowledge with blows.

"With your leave, Uncle Tomba: we've been
talking over two hours.   I must go on with the
lesson."

And while the shepherd, courteously dis-
missed, guided his sheep toward the mill to repeat his stories there, there began once again in
the school the chant of the multiplication-table
which was Don Joaquín's great symbol of learning.

At sunset, the boys sang their last song, thank-
ing the Lord "because He had helped them with
His light," and each one took up again his din-

ner-bag. As the distances in the *huerta* were not small, the youngsters would leave their homes in the morning with provisions enough to pass the whole day in school; and the enemies of Don Joaquín even said that one of his favourite punishments was to take away their rations in order thus to supplement the deficiencies of Doña Pepa's cooking.

Fridays, when school was out, the pupils invariably heard the same oration.

"Gentlemen: tomorrow is Saturday: remind your mothers and tell them that the one who does not bring his two coppers won't be let into the school. I tell you this particularly, Mr. de . . . So and So, and you, Mr. de . . . So and So" (and he would enumerate about a dozen names). "For three weeks now you have not brought the sum agreed upon, and if this goes on, it will prove that instruction is impossible, and learning impotent to combat the innate barbarity of these rustic regions. I contribute everything: my erudition, my books" (and he would glance at the three primer-charts, which his wife picked up carefully to put them away in the old bureau), "and you contribute nothing.   Well, what I said, I said: Any one who comes tomorrow empty-handed will not pass that threshold.   Notify your mothers."

The boys would form in couples, holding each other's hands (the same as in the schools of Valencia; what do you suppose?), and depart, after kissing the horny hand of Don Joaquín and repeating glibly as they passed near him:

"Good-bye, until tomorrow, by God's grace."

The master would accompany them to the little mill-square which was as a star for roads and paths; and there the formation was broken up into small groups and dispersed over different sections of the plain.

"Take care, my masters, I've got an eye on you," cried Don Joaquín as a last warning. "Look out when you steal fruit, throw stones or jump over canals.   I have a little bird who tells me everything and if tomorrow I hear anything bad, my rattan will play the very deuce with you."

And standing in the little square, he followed with his gaze the largest group which was departing up the Alboraya road.

These paid the best.   Among them walked the three sons of Batiste, for whom many a time

the road had been turned into a way of suffering.

Hand in hand the three tried to follow the other
boys, who because they lived in the farm-house
next to old Batiste, felt the same hatred as their
fathers for him and for his family and never
lost an opportunity to torment them.

The two elder ones knew how to defend themselves, and with a scratch more or less even came
out victorious at times.

But the smallest, Pascualet, a fat-stomached
little chap who was only five years old and
whom his mother adored for his sweetness and
gentleness, and hoped to make a chaplain, broke
into tears the moment he saw his brothers involved in deadly conflict with their fellow-pupils.

Many a time the two elder boys would reach
home covered with sweat and dust as though they
had been wallowing in the road, with their
trousers torn and their shirts unfastened. These
were the signs of combat; the little fellow told
it all with tears. And the mother had to minister
to one or another of the larger boys, which she
did by pressing a penny-piece on the bump raised
by some treacherous stone.

Teresa was much upset on hearing of the at-

tacks to which her son were subjected. But she
was a rough, courageous woman who had been
born in the country, and when she heard that
her boys had defended themselves well and
given a good thrashing to the enemy, she would
again regain her calm.

Good heaven! let them take care of Pascualet
first of all. And the oldest brother, indignant,
would promise a thrashing to all the lousy crew
when he met them on the roads.

Hostilities began every afternoon, as soon as
Don Joaquín lost sight of them.

The enemies, sons or nephews of those in the
tavern who threatened to put an end to Batiste,
began to walk more slowly, lessening the distance
between themselves and the three brothers.

The words of the master, however, and the
threat of the accursed bird who saw and told
everything, would still be ringing in their ears;
some laughed but on the wrong side of their
mouths. That old fellow knew such a lot!

But the farther off they got, the less effective
became the master's threat.

They would begin to prance around the three
brothers, and laughingly chase each other, a mere
malicious pretext, inspired by the instinctive hy-

pocrisy of youth, to push them as they ran by, with the pious desire of landing them in the canal that ran along the road.

Afterwards when this manœuvre proved unsuccessful, they would resort to slaps on the head and sudden pulls as they ran by at full speed.

"Thieves! Thieves!"

And as they hurled this insult, they would pull their ears and run off, only to turn after a little and repeat the same words.

This calumny, invented by the enemies of their father, made the boys absolutely frantic. The two older ones, abandoning Pascualet, who took refuge weeping behind a tree, would seize stones and a battle would begin in the middle of the road.

The cobbles whistled between the branches, making the leaves fall in showers, and bounce against the trunks and slopes: the dogs drawn by the noise of the battle, would rush out from the farm-houses barking fiercely, and the women from the doors of their houses would raise their arms to heaven, crying indignantly—

"Rascals! Devils!"

These scandals touched Don Joaquín to the quick and gave impetus next day to the relentless cane. What would people say of his school, the temple of good-breeding!

The battle would not end until some passing carter would brandish his whip, or until some old chap would come from the farm-houses, cudgel in hand, when the aggressors would flee, and disperse, repenting of their deed on seeing themselves alone, thinking fearfully, with the rapid shifting of impressions characteristic of childhood, of that bird who knew everything and of what Don Joaquín would have in store for them the following day.

And meanwhile, the three brothers would continue on their way, rubbing the bruises they had received in the battle.

One afternoon, Batiste's poor wife sent up a cry to heaven on seeing the state in which her young ones arrived.

The battle had been a fierce one! Ah! the bandits! The two older ones were bruised as usual; nothing to worry about.

But the little boy, the Bishop, as his mother called him caressingly, was wet from head to foot, and the poor little fellow was crying and trembling from cold and fear.

The savage young rascals had thrown him into

a canal of stagnant water and his brothers had fished him out covered with disgusting black mud.

The mother put him to bed, for the poor little chap was still trembling in her arms, clinging around her neck, and murmuring with a voice that sounded like the bleating of a lamb,

"Mother! Mother!"

"Lord God! give us patience!" All that base rabble, big and little, had resolved to put an end to the whole family.

VII

SAD and frowning as though he were going to a funeral, Batiste started forth one Thursday morning on the road to Valencia. It was horse-market day at the river-bed and the little bag of sackcloth containing the remainder of his savings bulged out his sash.

Misfortunes were pouring on the family in a steady stream. The last and fitting climax now would be that the roof should fall on their heads and crush them to death. What people! What a place had they got into!

The little boy was steadily getting worse, and trembled with fever in his mother's arms, while the latter wept continually. He was visited twice a day by the doctor; in short, it was a sickness which was going to cost twelve or fifteen dollars,—a mere trifle, so to speak.

The oldest boy, Batistet, could hardly go about. His head was still swathed in bandages and his face crisscrossed with scratches, after a

big battle which he had had one morning with
other boys of his own age who were going like
himself to gather manure in Valencia. All the
fematers (manure-gatherers) of the district had
banded against Batistet and the poor boy could
not show himself upon the road.

The two younger ones had stopped going to
school through fear of the fights that would be
forced on them on the way home.

And Roseta, poor girl! she was the saddest of
all. Her father put on a gloomy countenance
in the house, casting severe glances at her to remind her that she must not show her feelings
and that her sufferings were an outrage on paternal authority. But when he was alone, the
worthy Batiste felt grieved over the poor girl's
sadness. For he had once been young himself
and knew how heavy the sufferings of love may
be.

Everything had been discovered. After the
famous quarrel at the fountain of the Queen, the
whole *huerta* gossiped for days about Roseta's
love-affair with old Tomba's grandson.

The fat-bellied butcher of Alboraya stormed
angrily at his hired-man. Ah, the big rascal!
Now he knew why he forgot all his duties, why he

passed his afternoons wandering over the *huerta* like a gipsy. The young gentleman indulged himself in a fiancée, as though he had the means to support her. And what a fiancée, great Heaven! All he had to do was to listen to his customers as they chatted before his butcher's table. They all said the same: they were surprised that a man like him, religious and respectable, whose only defect was to cheat a little in the weight, should allow his hired-man to keep company with the daughter of the *huerta's* enemy, an evil man who, it was said, had been in the penitentiary.

And as all this to the mind of the fat boss was a dishonour to his establishment, he would become furious at every murmur of the gossiping women and threaten his timid hired-man with his knife, or reproach old Tomba as he tried to persuade him to reform his rascally grandson.

Finally the butcher discharged the boy and his grandfather found him a position in Valencia in another butcher-shop, where he asked them not to give him any time off even on holidays, so that he would not be able to wait for Batiste's daughter on the road.

Tonet departed submissively, his eyes wet like

one of the young lambs whom he had so often
dragged before the master's knife. He would
not return. The poor girl remained in the farm-
house, hiding herself in her bedroom to weep,
making efforts not to show her suffering to her
mother, who, exasperated by so many vexations,
was very intolerant, and before her father, who
threatened to kill her if she had another lover and
gave their enemies in the district any more
chance to talk.

Poor Batiste, who seemed so severe and threatening, was more grieved than by anything else at
the girl's inconsolable sorrow, her lack of appetite, her yellow complexion and hollow eyes, and
by the efforts she made to feign indifference, in
spite of the fact that she scarcely slept at all:
this, however, did not prevent her from trudging
off punctually every day to the factory with a
vagueness in her eyes which showed that her
mind was far afield, and that she lived perpetually in a state of inward dream.

Though they did not succeed in crushing Batiste, they undoubtedly cast on him the evil
eye, for his poor Morrut, the old horse who was
like a member of the family, who had drawn the
poor furniture and the youngsters over the roads

in the various peregrinations of poverty, gradually grew weaker and weaker in his new stable, the best lodging he had ever known in his long life of labour.

He had behaved like a respectable equine in the worst period, when the family had just moved to the farm, and he had had to plough up the land accursed and petrified by ten years' neglect; when he had had to plod continuously to Valencia to bring back débris and old boards from buildings being torn down; when the food was not plentiful and the work heavy. And now, when before the little window of the stable there stretched out a large field of grass, cool, high and waving, all for him; now that he had his table set with that green and juicy covering which smelled gloriously, now that he was growing fat, that his angular haunches and his bony back were rounding out, he died without even a reason, perhaps in the exercise of his perfect right to rest, after having helped the family through its time of trouble and tribulation.

He lay down one day on his straw and refused to go out, gazing at Batiste with glassy yellow eyes which silenced all angry oaths and threats upon the master's lips. Poor Morrut seemed to be a human being! Batiste, remembering his glance, felt like weeping. The farmhouse was all upset, and this misfortune for the time being made the family forget poor Pascualet, who was trembling with fever in his bed.

Batiste's wife was weeping. That poor beast whose gentle face lay there flat on the ground had seen almost all her children come into the world. She still remembered as though it were yesterday when they bought him in the Sagunto-market, small, dirty, covered with scabs, a nag condemned. It was a member of the family that was passing now. And when some repellent old men came in a cart to take the corpse of the old worker to the "boneyard" where they would convert his skeleton into bones of polished brilliancy and his flesh into fertilizer, the children wept, and called interminable farewells to poor Morrut who was carried away with his feet stretched out stiffly and his head swaying, while the mother, as though she felt some terrible presentiment, threw herself with open arms upon her sick little boy.

She saw her little son when he entered the stable to pull Morrut's tail, Morrut, who endured

all the youngster's pranks with affectionate submission. She saw the little fellow when his
father placed him on the animal's hard spine,
beating his little feet against the shining flanks
and crying, "Get up! Get up!" with his stammering child's voice. And she felt that the death
of the poor animal had somehow opened up a
way for others. Oh God! grant that her sorrowful mother's fears might be mistaken; that only
the long-suffering horse should die; and that he
should not, on his road to heaven, carry away
upon his flanks the poor little fellow now as in
other times he used to carry him along the paths
of the *huerta* grasping his mane, walking slowly
so as not to make him lose his balance!

And poor Batiste, his mind preoccupied by so
many misfortunes, confusing all together in his
fancy the sick child, the dead horse, the wounded
son and the daughter with her concentrated grief,
reached the outskirts of the city and passed over
the bridge of Serranos.

At the end of the bridge, on the esplanade between the two gardens in front of the octagonal
towers whose Gothic arcades, projecting barbi-
cans and noble crown of battlements rose above

the grove, Batiste stopped and passed his hands over his face.

He had to visit the masters, the sons of Don Salvador, and ask them to loan him a small sum to make up the necessary amount to buy a horse to take poor Morrut's place. And as cleanliness is the poor man's luxury, he sat down on a stone-bench, waiting his turn to have his beard shaved,—a two weeks' growth, stiff and bristly like porcupine-quills, which blackened his whole face.

In the shade of the high plane-trees, the barber-shops of the district, the open-air barbers as they were called, plied their trade. A couple of arm-chairs with rush-seats and arms made shiny by use, a portable furnace on which boiled the pot of water, towels of doubtful colour, and nicked razors which scraped the hard skin of the customers with raspings that made you shiver, constituted all the stock-in-trade of those open-air establishments.

Clumsy boys who aspired to be apprentices in the barber-shops of the town were there learning how to use their arms; and while they learned by inflicting cuts or by covering the victims'

heads with clips and bald-spots, the master con-
versed with the customers on the promenade-
bench or read the newspaper aloud to the group
who listened impassively.

As for those who sat on the chair of torment,
a piece of hard soap was rubbed over their jaws,
until the lather came. Then the cruel razor,
and cuts endured stoically by the customer, whose
face was tinged with blood. A little further on
resounded the enormous scissors in continuous
movement passing back and forth over the round
head of some vain youth, who was left shaved
like a poodle; the height of elegance, with a long
lock falling over the brow, and half the head
behind carefully cropped.

Batiste, swallowed up in the rush-chair, listened with closed eyes to the head-barber as he
read in a nasal and monotonous voice, and com-
mented and glossed like a man well versed in
public affairs. His shave resulted quite fortunately: all he got was three scrapes and a cut on
his ear. Other times there had been more. He
paid his half-real and departed; and entered the
city through the Serranos gate.

Two hours later he came out again and sat
down on the stone-bench among the group of

customers to listen to the head-barber until the time of the market arrived.

The masters had just loaned him the small amount he needed to buy the horse. The important thing now was to have a good eye in making his choice; to keep his temper and not let himself be cheated by the cunning gipsies who passed before him with their animals and went down the slope to the river-bed.

Eleven o'clock. The horse-market had evidently reached its moment of greatest animation. There came to Batiste's ears the confused sound of something like an invisible ebullition; the neighs of horses and voices of men rose from the river-bed. He hesitated, hung back, like a man who wants to put off an important resolution, and at last decided to go down to the market.

The river-bed as usual was dry. Some pools of water which had escaped from the water-wheels and dams which irrigated the plain wound in and out like serpents, forming curves and islands in a soil which was dusty, hot and uneven, more like an African desert than a river-bed.

At such times it was all white with sunlight, without the slightest spot of shade.

The carts of the farmers with their white awn-
ings formed an encampment in the middle of the
river-bed, and along the railing, placed in a
row, stood the horses which were for sale; the
black, kicking mules with their red caparisons
and their shining flanks all aquiver with nervous-
ness; the plough horses, strong and sad, like
slaves condemned to eternal labour, gazing with
glassy eyes at all those who passed as though they
divined in them the new tyrant, and the small
and lively nags, pawing up the dust and dragging
on the halter fastened to their nose-pieces.

Near the descent were the cast-off animals;
earless dirty donkeys; sad horses whose coat
seemed to be pierced by the sharp angles of
their fleshless bones; blind mules with long stork-
like necks; all the castaways of the market, the
wrecks of labour, whose hide had been well-
tanned by the stick and who awaited the arrival
of the contractor of bullfights or of the beggar
who still put them to some use.

Near the currents of water in the centre of the
river-bed, on the shores which dampness had
covered with a thin cloak of grassy sod, trotted
the colts who had not been broken, their long
manes flying in the wind, and their tails sweep-

ing the ground. Beyond the bridges, through the round stone "eyes" could be seen the herds of bulls with their legs drawn up, tranquilly ruminating the grass which the shepherds threw them, or stepping lazily over the hot ground, feeling the longing for green pastures and taking a fierce pose whenever the youngsters whistled to them from the railings.

The animation of the market was increasing. Around each horse whose sale was being arranged crowded groups of gesticulating and loquacious farmers in their shirt sleeves, their ashsticks in their hands. The thin, bronzed gipsies, with their long bowed legs, in sheepskin jackets covered with patches, and fur-caps beneath which their black eyes shone feverishly, talked ceaselessly, breathing into the faces of the customers as though they wished to hypnotize them.

"But just look at the horse! Notice her lines,—why, she's a beauty!"

And the farmer, impervious to the gipsy's honeyed phrases, reserved, thoughtful and uncertain, gazed at the ground, looked at the animal, scratched his head and finally said with a species of obstinate energy:

"All right . . . but I won't give any more."

To arrange the terms and solemnize the sales, the protection of a shed was sought, under which a big woman sold small cakes or filled sticky glasses with the contents of half a dozen bottles lined up on a zinc-covered table.

Batiste passed back and forth among the horses, paying no attention to the venders who pursued him, divining his intention.

Nothing pleased him. Alas, poor Morrut! How hard it was to find his successor! If he had not been compelled by necessity, he would have left without purchasing: he felt that it was an offence to the dead horse to fix his attention on these repellent beasts.

At last he stopped before a white nag, not very fat or sleek, with a few galls on his legs and a certain air of fatigue; a beast of burden who, though dejected, looked strong and will ing.

But scarcely had he passed his hand over the animal's haunches when he found at his side the gipsy, obsequious, familiar, treating him as though he had known him all his life.

"That animal is a treasure; it is easy to see that you know good horses when you see them . . . And cheap: I don't think we'll quarrel over the price . . . Monote! Walk him out so this gentleman can see what a graceful swing he has!"

And the Monote referred to, a little gipsy, took the horse by the halter and ran off with him over the uneven sand. The poor beast trotted after him reluctantly, as though bored by an operation that was so frequently repeated.

The curious people ran up and gathered around Batiste and the gipsy, who were gazing at the horse as it ran. When Monote returned with the animal Batiste examined it in detail; he put his fingers between the yellow teeth, passed his hands over his whole body, raised his hoofs to inspect them, and looked carefully between his legs.

"Look, look!" said the gipsy, . . . "he's just made for it. . . . Cleaner than the plate of the Eucharist. No one is cheated here; everything open and aboveboard. I don't fix up horses the way the others do who disfigure a burro before you can take your breath. I bought him last week and I even didn't fix up those trifles he has on the legs. You saw what a graceful swing he has. And for drawing a wagon? Why an elephant wouldn't have the push to him that he has! You can see the signs of it there on his neck."

Batiste did not look dissatisfied with his examination, but he tried to look displeased and made grimaces and rasped his throat. His misfortunes as a carter had given him knowledge of horses and he laughed inwardly at some of the curious ones who, influenced by the bad looks of the horse, were arguing with the gipsy, telling him that the horse was fit only to be sent to the boneyard. His sad and weary appearance was that of beasts of labour who obey as long as they can stand on their legs.

The moment of decision came. He would buy him. How much?

"Since it's for a friend," said the gipsy, touching his shoulder caressingly, "since it's for a nice fellow like you who will treat this jewel of a horse well, I'll let him go for forty dollars and the bargain's made."

Batiste received this broadside calmly, like a man well used to such discussions, and smiled slyly.

"Well, since it's you I'm dealing with, I won't offer you much less. Do you want twenty-five?"

The gipsy stretched out his arms with dramatic indignation, retreated a few steps, pulled at his fur cap, and made all kinds of extravagant and grotesque gestures to express his amazement.

"Mother of God! Twenty-five dollars! But did you look at the animal? Even if I had stolen him, I couldn't sell him at that price!"

But Batiste, to all his extravagant talk, always made the same reply:

"Twenty-five. Not a cent more."

And the gipsy, after exhausting all his persuasions, which were by no means few, fell back on the supreme argument.

"Monote . . . walk the horse out . . . so the gentleman can get a good look at him."

And away trotted Monote again, pulling the horse by the halter, more and more bored by all these promenadings.

"What a gait, hey?" said the gipsy. "You'd think he was a prince. Isn't he worth twenty-five dollars to to you?"

"Not a penny more," repeated the hard-headed Batiste.

"Monote . . . come back. That's enough."

And feigning indignation, the gipsy turned his back on the purchaser, intimating thereby that all the bargaining was off, but on seeing that Batiste was really leaving, his seriousness disappeared.

"Come, sir. . . . What's your name? . . .
Ah! Well, look, Mr. Batiste, so that you can
see that I like you and want you to own this
treasure, I'm going to do for you what I wouldn't
do for any one else. Do you agree to thirty-five
dollars? Come now, say yes. I swear to you
on your life that I wouldn't do as much for my
own father."

This time his protestations, on seeing that the
farmer was not moved by the reduction and offered him a beggarly two dollars more, were
even livelier and more gesticulatory than before.
Why, did that jewel of a horse inspire him with
no more liking than that? But man alive, hadn't
he eyes in his head to see his value? Come,
Monote; take him out again.

But Monote didn't have to tire himself out
again, for Batiste departed, pretending that he
had given up the purchase.

He wandered through the market looking at
other horses from afar, but always gazing out of
the tail of his eye at the gipsy, who similarly
feigning indifference, was following and watching him.

He approached a big, strong, sleek horse
which he did not think of buying, divining his

high price. He had scarcely passed his hand over the haunches when he felt a warm breath on his face, and heard the gipsy's voice murmuring:—

"Thirty-three. . . . On your children's lives, don't say no; you see I'm reasonable."

"Twenty-eight," said Batiste, without turning around.

When he grew tired of admiring that beautiful beast, he went on, and to have something to do, watched an old farmer's wife haggling over a donkey.

The first gipsy had gone back to his horse again, and was gazing at him from afar, and shaking the halter-rope as though he were calling him. Batiste slowly drew near him, pretending absent-mindedness, looking at the bridges over which passed the parasols of the women of the city, like many-coloured movable cupolas.

It was now noon. The sand of the river-bed grew hot; not the slightest breath of wind passed over the space between the railings. In that hot and sticky atmosphere, the sun beat down vertically penetrating the skin and burning the lips.

The gipsy advanced a few steps toward Batiste, offering him the end of the rope, as a kind of taking of possession.

"Neither your offer nor mine.   Thirty, and God knows I get no profit on it.   Thirty . . . don't say no, or you'll make me wild.   Come, put it there!"

Batiste took the rope and offered his hand to the vender who pressed it with much feeling. The bargain was concluded.

The former began to take from his sash all that plethora of savings which swelled out his stomach like an undigested meal: a bank-note that the master had loaned him, a few silver dollars, a handful of small change wrapped up in a paper-cone.   When the count was completed, he could not get out of going with the gipsy to the shed to invite him to take a drink, and giving a few pennies to Monote for all his trottings.

"You're carrying off the treasure of the market.   It's a lucky day for you, Mist' Bautista: you crossed yourself with your right hand, and the Virgin came out to look at you."

And he had to drink a second glass, the gipsy's treat, but at last, cutting short his torrent of

offers and flatteries, he seized the halter of his
new horse and helped by the obliging Monote,
mounted on the steed's bare back and left the
noisy market at a trot.

He departed well satisfied with the animal;
he had not lost his day. He scarcely remembered poor Morrut, and he felt the pride of
ownership when on the bridge and on the road,
some one from the *huerta* turned around to
examine the white steed.

But his greatest satisfaction came when he
passed before the house of Copa. He made the
beast break into an arrogant little trot as though
he were a horse of pedigree, and he saw how
Pimentó and all the loafers of the *huerta* came
to the door to look after him; the wretches!
Now they would be convinced that it was diffi-
cult to crush him, and that by his unaided efforts,
he could defend himself. Now they saw that
he had a new horse. If only the trouble within
the home could be as easily adjusted!

His high, green wheat formed a kind of lake
of restless waves by the roadside; the alfalfa-
grass grew luxuriantly and had a perfume which
made the horse's nostrils dilate. Batiste could
not complain of his land, but it was inside

the house that he feared to meet misfortune,
eternal companion of his existence, waiting to
dig its claws into him.

On hearing the trotting of the horse, Batistet
came out with his bandaged head, and ran to
hold the animal while his father dismounted.
The boy waxed enthusiastic over the new animal.
He caressed him, put his hands between his lips,
and in his eagerness to get on his back, he put
one foot on the hook, seized his tail and mounted
with the agility of an Arab on his crupper.

Batiste entered the house. As white and
clean as usual, with its shining tiles and all the
furniture in its place, it seemed to be enveloped
in the sadness of a clean and shining sepulchre.

His wife came out to the door of the room,
her eyes red and swollen and her hair dishevelled, revealing in her tired aspect the long,
sleepless nights she had spent.

The doctor had just gone away: as usual, little hope. His manner was forbidding, he spoke
in half-words, and after examining the boy a
little, he went out without leaving any new
prescription. Only when he mounted his horse,
he had said that he would return at night. And
the child was the same, with a fever that con-

sumed his little body, which grew thinner and thinner.

It was the same thing every day. They had grown accustomed now to that misfortune; the mother wept automatically, and the others went about their usual occupations with sad faces.

Then Teresa, who had a business head, asked her husband about the result of his journey; she wanted to see the horse; and even sad Roseta forgot her sorrows of love and inquired about the new acquisition.

All, large and small, went to the barnyard to see the horse in his stable; Batistet full of enthusiasm had brought him there. The child remained abandoned in the big bed of the bedroom where he tossed about, his eyes glazed with sickness, bleating weakly: "Mother! Mother!"

Teresa examined her husband's purchase with a grave expression, calculating in detail whether he was worth more than thirty dollars; the daughter sought out the differences between the new horse and Morrut of happy memory, and the two youngsters, with sudden confidence, pulled his tail and stroked his belly, and vainly begged their older brother to put them up on his white back.

Everybody was decidedly pleased with this new member of the family, who sniffed the manger in an odd way as though he found there some trace, some remote odour of his dead companion.

The whole family had dinner, and the excitement and enthusiasm over the new acquisition was such that several times Batistet and the little ones slipped away from the table to go and take a look in the stable, as though they feared the horse had sprouted wings and flown away.

The afternoon passed without anything happening. Batiste had to plough up a part of the land which he was keeping uncultivated, preparing the crop of garden-truck, and he and his son put the horse in harness, proud to see the gentleness with which he obeyed and the strength with which he drew the plough.

At nightfall, when they were about to return, Teresa called them, screaming from the farmhouse door, and her voice was like that of one who is crying for help.

"Batiste!—Batiste!—Come quickly!"

And Batiste ran across the field, frightened by the tone of his wife's voice and by her wild actions; for she was tearing her hair and moaning.

The child was dying; you had only to see him to be convinced of it. Batiste entered the bedroom and leaning over the bed, felt a shudder of cold go over him, a sensation as though some one had just thrown a stream of cold water on him from behind. The poor little Bishop scarcely moved; he breathed stertorously and with difficulty; his lips grew purple; his eyes, almost closed, showed the glazed and motionless pupil; they were eyes which saw no more; and his little brown face seemed to be darkened by a mysterious sadness as though the wings of death cast their shadow on it. The only bright thing in that countenance was the blond hair streaming over the pillows like a skein of curly silk; the flame of the candle shone on it strangely.

The mother's groans were desperate; they were like the howlings of a maddened beast. Her son, weeping silently, had to check her, to hold her in order to keep her from throwing herself on the little one or dashing her head against the wall. Outside the youngsters were weeping, not daring to come in, as though the lamentations of the mother frightened them, and by the side of the bed stood Batiste, absorbed, clenching his fists, biting his lips, his eyes fixed on that little body, which it was costing so much anguish, so many shudders, to give up its hold on life. The calm of that giant, his dry eyes winking nervously, his head bent down toward his son, gave an even more painful impression than the lamentations of the mother.

Suddenly, he noticed that Batistet stood by his side; he had followed him, alarmed by his mother's cries. Batiste was angry when he found out that his son had left the horse alone in the middle of the field, and the boy, drying his eyes, ran out to bring the horse back to the stable.

In a short while, new cries awakened Batiste from his stupor.

"Father! Father!"

It was Batistet calling him from the door of the farm-house. The father, foreseeing some new misfortune, ran after him, not understanding his confused words. "The horse . . . the poor white horse . . . lay on the ground . . . blood. . . ."

And after a few steps he saw him lying on

his haunches, still harnessed to the plough but trying in vain to rise, stretching out his neck and neighing dolorously, while from his side, near one of his forelegs, a black liquid trickled slowly, soaking the freshly opened furrows.

They had wounded him; perhaps he was going to die. God! A beast that he needed like his own life and which had cost him money borrowed from the master.

He looked around as though seeking the perpetrator of the deed. There was no one on the plain, which was growing purple in the twilight; nothing could be heard but the far-off rumbling of wheels, the rustling noise of the canebrakes, and the cries of people calling from one farm-house to another. In the near-by roads, on the paths, there was not a single soul.

Batistet tried to excuse himself to his father for negligence. While he was running toward the farmhouse, he had seen a group of men coming along the road, gay people who were laughing and singing, returning doubtless from the inn. Perhaps it was they.

The father would not listen to anything more. . . . Pimentó, who else could it be? The hatred of the district had caused his son's death, and now that thief was killing his horse, guessing how much he needed it. God! Was that not enough to make a Christian turn to evil ways?

And he argued no more. Scarcely realizing what he was doing, he returned to the farmhouse, seized his musket from behind the door, and ran out, mechanically opening the breech to see if the two barrels were loaded.

Batistet remained near the horse, trying to staunch the blood with the bandage from his own head. He was fear-stricken when he saw his father running along the road with his musket cocked, longing to give vent to his rage by slaying.

It was terrible to see that big, quiet, slow man in whom the wild beast, tired of being daily harassed, was now awakened. In his bloodshot eyes burned a murderous light; all his body trembled with anger, that terrible anger of the peaceful man who, when he passes the boundaries of gentleness, becomes ferocious.

Like a furious wild boar, he entered the fields, trampling down the plants, jumping over the irrigation streams, breaking off the canes; if he diverged from the road, it was only to reach Pimentó's farm more quickly.

Some one was at the door. The blindness of anger and the twilight shadows prevented him from distinguishing if it was a man or a woman, but he saw how the person with one leap sprang in and closed the door suddenly, frightened by that vision on the point of raising his gun and firing.

Batiste stopped before the closed door of the farm-house:

"Pimentó! . . . Thief! Come out!"

And his voice amazed him as though it was another's.

It was a voice which was trembling and shrill, high-pitched and suffocated by anger.

No one answered. The door remained closed; closed the windows and the three loopholes at the top which lighted the upper story, the *cambra*, where the crops were kept.

The scoundrel was probably gazing at him through some crack, perhaps even cocking his gun to fire some treacherous shot from one of the high small windows. And instinctively, with that foresight of the Moor always alert in suspecting all kinds of evil tricks of the enemy, he hid behind the trunk of a giant fig-tree which cast its shade over Pimentó's house.

The latter's name resounded ceaslessly in the silence of the twilight accompanied by all kinds of insults.

"Come down! You coward! Come out, you thug!"

And the farm-house remained silent and closed, as though it had been abandoned.

Batiste thought he heard a woman's stifled cries; the noise of a struggle; something which made him suppose a fight was going on between poor Pepeta and Pimentó, whom she was trying to prevent from going out to answer the insults; but after that he heard nothing, and his insults reverberated in a silence which made him desperate.

This infuriated him more than if the enemy had shown himself. He felt himself going mad. It seemed to him that the mute house was mocking him, and abandoning his hiding-place, he threw himself against the door, striking it with the butt of his gun.

The timbers trembled with the pounding of the infuriated giant. He wished to vent his rage on the dwelling, since he could not annihilate the master, and not only did he beat the door, but he also struck his gun against the walls, dislodging enormous pieces of plaster. Several times, he even raised the weapon to his face, wishing to fire his two shots at the two little windows of the *cambra,* and was deferred from this only by his fear that he would remain disarmed.

His anger increased; he roared forth insults; his bloodshot eyes could scarcely see; he staggered like a drunken man. He was almost on the point of falling to the ground in a fit of apoplexy, agonized with anger, choked by fury, when suddenly the red clouds which surrounded him tore themselves apart, his fury gave way to weakness, he saw all his misfortune, felt himself crushed; his anger, broken by the terrible tension, vanished, and Batiste, amidst the torrent of insults, felt his voice grow stifled till it became a moan, and at last he burst out crying.

And he stopped insulting Pimentó. He began gradually to retreat, till he reached the road, and sat down on a bank, his musket at his feet. There he wept and wept, feeling a great relief, caressed by the shadows of night which seemed to share his sorrow, for they became deeper, deeper, hiding his childish weeping.

How unfortunate he was! Alone against all! He would find the little fellow dead when he re-

turned to the farm; the horse which was his livelihood made useless by those traitors; trouble
coming on him from every direction, surging up
from the roads, from the houses, from the canebrakes, profiting by all occasions to wound him
and his; and he defenceless, could not protect
himself from these enemies who vanished the
moment, weary of suffering, he tried to turn on
them.

Lord! what had he done to deserve such sufferings?   Was he not an honest man?

He felt himself more and more crushed by
grief.   Unable to move he remained seated on
the bank; his enemies might come; he had not
even the strength to pick up the musket that lay at
his feet.

Over the road resounded the slow tolling of a
bell which filled the darkness with mysterious vi-
brations.   Batiste thought of his little boy, of the
poor "Bishop" who probably had died by now.
Perhaps that sweet chime was made by the angels who came down from heaven to bear the
child's soul away; and who unable to find his
farm were flying over the *huerta*.   If only the
others did not remain, those who needed the
strength of his arm to support them! . . . The

poor man longed for annihilation; he thought of
the happiness of leaving down there on that bank,
that ugly body, the life of which it cost him so
much to sustain, and embracing the innocent little
soul of his boy, of flying away like the blessèd
ones whom he had seen guided by angels in the
paintings of the church.

The chimes seemed to approach and dark figures which his tear-wet eyes could not distinguish
passed by on the road. He felt some one touch
him with the end of a stick and, raising his head,
he saw a solitary figure, a kind of spectre leaning toward him.

And he recognized old Tomba, the only one of
the *huerta* to whom he owed no suffering.

The shepherd, considered as a sorcerer, possessed the amazing intuition of the blind.
Scarcely had he recognized Batiste when he
seemed to understand all his misfortune. He
felt with his stick the musket lying at his feet, and
turned his head, as though looking for Pimentó's
farm in the darkness.

He spoke slowly, with a quiet sadness, like a
man accustomed to the miseries of a world which
he must soon leave. He divined that Batiste was
weeping.

"My son . . . my son. . . ."

He had expected everything that had occurred. He had warned him the first day when he saw him settled on the accursed lands. They would bring him misfortune.

He had just passed by Batiste's farm and had seen lights through the open door . . . he had heard cries of despair; the dog was howling . . . the little boy had died, hadn't he? And he yonder, thinking he was seated on a bank, when in reality he sat with one foot in prison. Thus men are lost and their families broken up. He would end with some mad and foolish murder, like poor Barret, and would die like him, in prison. It was inevitable; those lands were cursed by the poor and could give forth only accursed fruits.

And muttering his terrible prophecies, the shepherd went his way behind his sheep on the village road, advising poor Batiste to leave also, and go away, very far away, where he could earn his bread without having to struggle against the hatred of the poor. And now invisible, shrouded in the shadows, Batiste still heard his slow, sad voice which made him shudder:

"Believe me, my son . . . they will bring you misfortune!"

VIII

BATISTE and his family did not realize how the unheard-of, unexpected event began; who was the first who decided to pass the bridge that joined the road to the hated fields.

In the farm-house they were in no condition to notice such details. Exhausted with suffering, they saw that the people of the *huerta* had suddenly begun to come to them, and they did not protest, for misfortune needs counsel, nor did they offer thanks for the unexpected impulse to approach.

The news of the little boy's death had been transmitted through all the neighbourhood with the strange swiftness with which all news spreads in the *huerta*, flying from farm to farm on the wings of scandal, which is the swiftest of all telegraphs.

Many slept poorly that night. It seemed as though the little boy, as he departed, had left a thorn fixed in the consciences of the neighbours.

More than one woman tossed about in bed, disturbing with her restlessness her husband's sleep, making him protest indignantly. "But curse you! will you go to sleep? . . ." No, she couldn't; that child prevented her from sleeping. Poor little fellow! What would he tell the Lord when he reached Heaven?

All shared the responsibility of that death, but each one with hypocritical egotism attributed to his neighbour the chief blame for the bitter persecution whose consequences had fallen on the little fellow's head; each gossiping woman blamed her enemy for the deed. And at last she went to sleep with the intention of undoing all the evil done, of going in the morning to offer her aid to the family, of weeping over the poor child; and amid the mists of sleep they thought they saw Pascualet, as white and resplendent as an angel, looking with reproachful eyes at those who had been so hard with him and his family.

All the people of the neighbourhood rose meditating as to how they could approach and enter Batiste's house. It was an examination of conscience, an explosion of repentance which burst on the poor farm-house from every end of the plain.

It had scarcely dawned when two old women
who lived in a neighbouring farm-house entered
Batiste's home. The family, crushed with
grief, felt almost no wonder at seeing those two
women appear in the house which no one had
entered for more than six months.   They wanted
to see the child, the poor little "Bishop," and entering the bedroom they gazed at him still lying
there in the bed; the edge of the sheet pulled up
to his chin scarcely outlining the shape of his
body, his blond head inert and heavy on the pillow.   The mother could only weep in her corner, all shrunken and crouched together, as small
as a child, as though she were trying to annihilate herself and disappear.

After these women came others and still
others; it was a stream of weeping old women
who arrived from all parts of the plain; surrounding the bed, they kissed the little corpse
and seemed to take possession of him as their
own, leaving Teresa and her daughter aside; the
latter, exhausted by lack of sleep and weeping,
seemed imbecile as they hung their red and tear-
wet faces on their breasts.

Batiste, seated in a rush-chair, in the middle
of the farm-house, gazed stupidly at that proces-

sion of people who had so ill-treated him. He did not hate them, but neither did he feel gratitude. He had come forth from the crisis of the day before crushed, and he gazed at all this with indifference, as though the farm-house were not his, as though the poor little fellow on the bed were not his son.

Only the dog curling up at his feet seemed to remember and feel hatred: he sniffed hostilely at all the procession of petticoats that came and went, and growled as though he wanted to bite and only refrained from doing so in order not to displease his masters.

The young people shared the dog's resentment. Batistet scowled at all those old women who had made fun of him so often when he passed before their houses, and he took refuge in the stable so as not to lose sight of the poor horse, whom he was curing according to the instructions of the veterinary, called in the night before. He was very fond of his little brother; but death has no remedy, and what he was anxious about now was that the horse should not be permanently lame.

The two little ones, pleased in their hearts at a misfortune which attracted to their house the attention of the whole plain, kept watch over the door, barring the way to the small boys who like bands of sparrows arrived by all roads and paths with morbid and excited curiosity to see the little body of the dead child. Now *their* turn had come; now *they* were the masters. And with the courage of those who are in their own homes, they threatened and drove away some and let others enter, giving them their favour according to the treatment they had received from them in the bloody vicissitudes of their peregrinations on their way home from school. . . . Rascals! There were even some who insisted on entering after having played a part in the battle during which poor Pascualet had fallen into the canal, thus catching the illness which had been his death.

The appearance of a weak, pale little woman seemed to bring suddenly on the whole family a host of painful recollections. It was Pepeta, Pimentó's wife! Even she came!

An impulse of protestation came over both Batiste and his wife. But to what purpose? Welcome, and if she entered to enjoy their misfortune, she could laugh as much as she wished. There they were all inert, crushed by grief.

God, the all-seeing, would give to every one his deserts.

But Pepeta went straight to the bed, pushing the other women aside. She bore in her arms an enormous bunch of flowers and leaves which she spread out upon the bed. The first perfumes of the nascent springtime spread through the room which smelled of medicine, and in whose heavy atmosphere insomnia and sighs of desperation seemed to be inhaled.

Pepeta, the poor beast of burden, dead for maternity though married with the hope of becoming a mother, lost her calm on seeing that little marble face, framed in the turned-back hair as in a nimbus of gold.

"My son! . . . my poor little boy!"

And she wept with all her soul, as she bent over the little corpse, barely grazing with her lips the pale, cold brow, as though she feared to awaken him.

On hearing her sobs, Batiste and his wife raised their heads in astonishment. They knew now that she was a good woman: *he* was the bad one. And a mother's and father's gratitude shone in their eyes.

Batiste even trembled when he saw how poor

Pepeta embraced Teresa and her daughter, and mingled her tears with theirs. No; here was no duplicity. She herself was a victim; that was why she could understand the misfortunes of others who were also victims.

The little woman wiped away her tears, and became again the brave, strong woman accustomed to the labour of a beast of burden to keep up her house. She cast an amazed glance around. Things could not stay like that. The child in the bed and everything in disorder! The "Bishop" must be laid out for his last journey, he must be dressed in white, pure and resplendent as the dawn, whose name he bore.

And with the instinct of a superior being born for practical life, with the power of imposing obedience on others, she began to give orders to all the women who vied in doing some service for the family they had hitherto cursed so vehemently.

She would go to Valencia with two companions to buy the shroud and the coffin. Others went to the village, or scattered about among the neighbouring farm-houses in search of the objects which Pepeta charged them to procure.

Even the hateful Pimentó who remained invisible, had to contribute to these preparations. His wife met him on the road and ordered him to look for some musicians for the evening. They were, like himself, vagabonds and drunkards; he would certainly find them at Copa's. And the bully, who seemed preoccupied that day, listened to his wife's words without reply and endured the imperious tone in which she spoke to him, gazing down at the ground as though ashamed.

Since the previous night he felt himself transformed. That man who had defied and insulted him and kept him shut up in his own house like a timid hen; his wife, who for the first time had imposed her will upon him and taken his musket away; his lack of courage to face his victim, who was wholly in the right; all these reasons kept him confused and crushed.

He was no longer the Pimentó of other days; he began to know himself and even to suspect that all the things done against Batiste and his family amounted to a crime. There even came a moment when he despised himself. What a man he was! . . . All the mean tricks of himself and the other neighbours had served only to take the life of a poor child. And as was his custom in dark days, when some trouble made him frown, he marched off to the tavern, seeking the consolations that Copa kept in his famous wine-barrel in the corner.

At ten in the morning, when Pepeta and her two companions returned from the city, the house was filled with people.

Some men who were very slow and heavy and domestic, who had taken little part in the crusade against the strangers, formed a group with Batiste in the door of the farm-house; some squatting, in Moorish fashion, others seated in rush-chairs, smoking and speaking slowly of the weather and the crops.

Inside, women and more women, pressing around the bed, deafening the mother with their talk; some speaking of the sons they had lost, others installed in corners as though they were in their own homes, gossiping about all the rumours of the neighbourhood. That day was extraordinary; it made no difference that their houses were dirty and that dinner must be cooked; there was an excuse. The children clinging to their skirts wept and deafened everybody with their cries, some wanting to return home, others begging to be shown the "Bishop."

Some old women took possession of the cupboard and every moment prepared big glasses of sugared wine and water, offering them to Teresa and her daughter so they could weep more comfortably, and when the poor creatures, swollen by this sugary inundation, declined to drink, the officious old gossips took turns in swallowing the refreshments themselves, for they also needed to recover from their sorrow.

Pepeta began to shout, desirous of inspiring respect in this confusion. "Go away, all of you!" Instead of staying here and bothering people, they ought to take the two poor women away with them, for they were exhausted with sorrow and driven crazy by so much noise.

Teresa objected to abandoning her son even for a short time; she would soon see him no more; they should not steal from her any of the time that remained to her to look upon her treasure. And bursting out into even greater lamentations, she threw herself on the cold corpse, wishing to embrace it.

But the supplications of her daughter and Pepeta's will were stronger, and Teresa, escorted by a great number of women, left the farm-house with her apron over her face, moaning, staggering, heedless of those who pulled her away with them, each one vying with the other as to who should take her home.

Pepeta began to arrange the funeral cere‐ mony. She placed in the centre of the entrance the little white table on which the family ate, and covered it with a sheet, fastening the ends with pins.   On it they placed a quilt which was starched and lace-trimmed, and there they placed the little coffin brought from Valencia, a jewel of a coffin which the neighbours admired; a white casket trimmed with gold braid, padded inside like a baby's cradle.

Pepeta took out of a bundle the last finery of the dead child; the shroud of gauze woven of silver thread, the sandals, the garland of flowers, all white, whose purity was symbolic of that of the poor little "Bishop."

Slowly, with maternal care, Pepeta shrouded the corpse. She pressed the cold little body against her breast, introduced into the shroud, with the greatest care, the rigid little arms, as though they were bits of glass which might be broken at the least shock, and kissed the icy feet before putting them into the sandals.

In her arms, like a white dove stiff with cold,

she carried Pascualet to the casket; to that altar raised in the middle of the farm-house before which the whole *huerta,* drawn by curiosity, would defile.

Nor was this all: the best was still lacking, the garland, a bonnet of white flowers with festoons which hung over the ears; a barbaric adornment like those worn by savages at the opera. Pepeta's pious hand, engaged in a terrible struggle with death, stained the pale cheeks a rosy colour; the mouth, blackened by death, she toned up with a layer of bright scarlet, but her efforts to open the weak eyelids wide were vain; they kept falling, covering the dull filmed eyes, eyes without lustre, which had the grey sadness of death.

Poor Pascualet . . . unhappy little Bishop! With his grotesque garland and his painted face, he was turned into a ridiculous scarecrow. He had inspired more sorrowful tenderness when his pale little face had been livid in death on his mother's pillow, adorned only with his own blond hair.

But all this did not prevent the good women of the *huerta* from admiring Pepeta's work en-

thusiastically. Look at him, . . . why, he
seemed to be asleep! So beautiful, so pinkly
flushed! . . . never had such a little Abbot
been seen before.

And they filled the hollows of his casket with
flowers; flowers on the white vestment, scattered
on the table, piled up in clusters at the ends; the
whole plain's luxuriance embraced the child's
body, which it had so often seen running along
its paths like a bird; enveloped it with a wave of
colour and perfume.

The two small brothers gazed on Pascualet
astonished, piously, as on a superior being who
might take flight at any time; the dog prowled
around the catafalque stretching out his muzzle
to lick the cold, waxen, little hands, and burst
out into an almost human lamentation, a moan
of despair which made the women nervous and
impelled them to chase the poor beast away with
kicks.

At noon, Teresa, escaping almost by main
force from the captivity in which her neighbours
kept her, returned home. Her mother-love filled
her with a feeling of deep satisfaction when she
beheld the little fellow's finery; she kissed his

painted mouth and redoubled her lamentations.

It was dinner-time. Batistet and the little ones, whose grief did not succeed in killing their appetites, devoured a broken crust, hidden in the corners. Teresa and her daughter had no thought of food. The father, still seated in his rush-chair, smoked cigar after cigar, impassive as an Oriental, turning his back on his dwelling as if he feared to see the white catafalque which served as an altar for his son's body.

In the afternoon, the visitors were more numerous. The women arrived, decked out in holiday attire, and wearing their mantillas for the funeral; the girls disputed energetically as to who should be one of the four to carry the poor little Bishop to the cemetery.

Walking slowly by the edge of the road and avoiding the dust as though it were a deadly danger, some distinguished visitors arrived: Don Joaquín and Doña Josefa, the schoolmaster and the "lady." That afternoon, because of the unhappy event (as he declared), there was no school, as was very evident, from the crowd of bold and sticky boys who slipped into the farm-house, and tired of contemplating the corpse of their erstwhile companion as they picked at their noses, came out to run around on the nearby road or to jump over the canals.

Doña Josefa, in a threadbare woollen dress and a large yellow mantilla, entered the farmhouse silently, and after a few pompous phrases caught from her husband, seated her robust self in a large rope-chair and remained as mute as if asleep, in contemplation of the coffin. The good woman, accustomed to hearing and admiring her husband, could not carry on a conversation by herself.

The schoolmaster, who was showing off his short green jacket which he wore on days of ceremony, and his necktie of gigantic proportions, sat down outside by the father's side. His big farmer's hands were encased in black gloves which had grown grey in the course of years, till now they were the colour of a fly's wing; he moved them constantly, desirous of drawing attention to the garments he wore on occasions of great solemnity.

For Batiste's benefit, he brought out the most flowery and high-sounding phrases of his repertory. The latter was his best customer; not a single Saturday had he failed to give his sons the two coppers for the school.

"It's life, Mr. Bautista; resignation. We never know God's plans. Often he turns evil into good for his creatures."

And interrupting his string of commonplaces, uttered pompously as though he were in school, he lowered his voice and added, blinking his eyes maliciously:

"Did you notice, Mr. Batiste, all these people? Yesterday they were cursing you and your family; and God knows how many times I have censured them for this wickedness; today they enter your house as though they were entering their own, and overwhelm you with manifestations of affection. Misfortune makes them forget, brings them close to you."

And after a pause, during which he stood with lowered head, he added with conviction, striking his breast:

"Believe me, for I know them well; at bottom they are very good people. Very stupid, certainly. Capable of the most barbarous actions, but with hearts which are moved by misfortune and which make them draw in their claws. . . . Poor people! Whose fault is it that they were born stupid and that no one tries to help them to overcome it?"

He was silent for some time, and then he added with the fervour of a merchant praising his article:

"What is necessary here is education, much education. Temples of wisdom to spread the light of knowledge over this plain; torches which . . . which . . . In short, if more youngsters came to my temple, I mean to my school, and if the fathers, instead of getting drunk paid punctually like you, Mr. Bautista, things would be different. And I say nothing more, for I don't like to offend."

There was danger of this, for many of the fathers who sent him pupils unballasted by the two pennies were near.

Other farmers, those who had shown the family the most hostility, did not dare to approach the house, and remained grouped together on the road.

Among them was Pimentó, who had just arrived from the tavern with five musicians, his conscience easy after remaining a few hours near Copa's counter.

More and more people poured into the farmhouse. There was no free space left in it, and the women and children sat on the brick-benches beneath the vine-arbour or on the slopes, waiting for the hour set for the funeral.

Within were heard lamentations, counsels energetically uttered, the noise of a struggle. It was Pepeta, trying to separate Teresa from her son's body. Come! . . . she must be reasonable; the "Bishop" could not stay there for ever, it was getting late, and it was better to drink the bitter cup down and get it over with.

And she struggled with the mother to make her leave the coffin and enter the bedroom, so as not to be present at the terrible moment of departure, when the "Bishop" would rise and take flight on the white wings of his shroud never to return.

"My son! his mother's darling!" moaned poor Teresa.

She would see him no more; one kiss, another; and the head, more and more marblelike and livid despite the paint, moved from one side of the pillow to the other, making the diadem of flowers shake in the anxious hands of the mother and sister who disputed the last kiss.

At the end of the village the vicar would be found with the sacristan and the acolytes: they must not be kept waiting. Pepeta was growing impatient. Inside! Inside! And aided by other women, Teresa and her daughter were installed almost by main force in the bedroom, and walked up and down with dishevelled hair and eyes, red with weeping, their breasts heaving with a protest of sorrow which expresed itself not with moans but with howls.

Four girls with hoop-skirts, their silk mantillas falling over their eyes, and who had a modest and nun-like expression, seized the legs of the little table, raising all the white catafalque. Like the salvos saluting the flag as it is raised, there resounded a strange, prolonged, terrifying moan, which made chills run down the backs of many. It was the dog taking leave of the poor "Bishop," uttering an interminable lamentation, tears in his eyes and paws outstretched as if he wished himself to follow his very cry.

Outside, Don Joaquín was clapping his hands to command attention. Come now . . . let the whole school form! The people on the road had approached the farm-house. Pimentó captained the musicians; the latter prepared their instruments to salute the "Bishop" as soon as the coffin should pass the threshold, and amid the disorder and shouts with which the procession formed, the clarinet trilled, the cornet played, and the trombone blew like a fat, asthmatic old man.

The youngsters started out, raising high great bunches of sweet basil. Don Joaquín knew how to do things properly. Afterward, breaking through the crowd, appeared the four damsels holding the light, white altar on which the poor "Bishop," lying in his coffin, moved his head with a slight movement from side to side as though he were taking leave of the farm-house.

The musicians burst forth into a playful, merry waltz, taking up their position behind the bier, and behind them, all the curious people ran along the little road to the farm in compact groups.

The farm-house remained mute and dark, with that melancholy atmosphere of places over which misfortune has passed.

Batiste, alone under the vine-arbour, still in his attitude of an impressive Arab, bit his cigar and followed the course of the procession which began to wind along the highway, the coffin and its catafalque looking like an enormous white dove among the black robes and green branches which marked the cortège.

Auspiciously did the poor "Bishop" set out upon his way to the heaven of the innocents. The plain, stretching out voluptuously under the kiss of the springtime sun, enveloped the dead child with its fragrance, accompanied him to the tomb, and covered him with an imperceptible shroud of perfumes. The old trees, which had germinated, filled with the sap of new life, seemed to greet the little corpse as they moved in the breeze, their branches heavy-laden with flowers. Never had Death passed over the earth so beautiful a mask.

Dishevelled and screaming like madwomen, waving their arms furiously, the two unhappy women appeared in the door of the farm-house, their voices prolonged like an interminable moan in the quiet atmosphere of the plain, pervaded with soft light.

"My son! . . . My soul! . . ." moaned poor Teresa and her daughter.

Nnnnn! nnnnn! howled the dog, stretching out his muzzle in a long groan, which set the nerves on edge and seemed to send a funereal shiver over all the plain.

"Good-bye, Pascualet! . . . Good-bye!" cried
the little ones, swallowing their tears.

And from afar, among the foliage, borne over
the green waves of the fields, replied the echoes
of the valley, accompanying the poor "Bishop"
to eternity, as he swayed back and forth in his
white barge trimmed with gold. The complicated scales of the cornet, with its diabolic
capers, seemed like a happy outburst of laughter
from Death, who with the child in her arms, departed amid the sunset resplendencies of the
plain.

At evening-fall, the procession returned home.

The little ones, sleepy from the excitement of
the preceding night, when Death had visited
them, slept in their chairs. Teresa and her
daughter, overcome by weeping, their energy
exhausted after so many sleepless nights, were
prostrated. They fell on the bed which still
showed signs of the poor child's body, while Batistet snored in the stable near the sick horse.

The father, still silent and impassive, received
visitors, shook hands, and gave thanks with
movements of the head to the offers and con-
solatory expressions.

When the night shut in, all had gone.

The farm-house remained dark and silent.
Through the murky open door there came, like
a far-off whisper, the weary breathing of the
tired family, all of whom had fallen exhausted
as though slain in the battle of grief.

Batiste, still motionless, gazed stupefied at the
stars which twinkled in the dark blue of night.

Solitude brought him to his senses; he began
to realize his situation.

The plain had its usual aspect, but to him it
appeared more beautiful, more tranquillizing,
like a frowning face which unbends and smiles.

The people, whose shouts resounded in the
distance in the doors of the farm-houses, no
longer hated him and would no longer persecute
his children. They had been beneath his roof
and had blotted out with their footsteps the curse
that lay on the lands of old Barret. He would
begin a new life. But at what a price!

And suddenly facing the exact realization of
his misfortune, thinking of poor Pascualet, who
now lay crushed by a heavy weight of damp and
fetid earth, his white vestment contaminated by
the corruption of other bodies, ambushed by the
filthy worm, the beautiful boy with the delicate
skin over which his calloused hand had been

wont to glide, the blond hair which he had so often caressed, he felt a leaden wave which rose from his stomach to his throat.

The crickets which sang on the nearby slope grew silent, frightened by the strange hiccough which broke the stillness, and sounded in the darkness for the greater part of the night like the stertorous breathing of a wounded beast.

IX

S T. JOHN'S day arrived, the greatest period
of the year; the time of harvest and abundance.

The air vibrated with light and colour. An
African sun poured torrents of gold upon the
earth, cracking it with its ardent caresses, and its
arrows of gold slipped in between the compressed foliage, an awning of verdure under
which the *vega* protected its babbling canals and
its humid furrows, as though fearful of the heat
which generated life everywhere.

The trees showed their branches loaded with
fruit. The medlar trees bent over under the
weight of the yellow clusters covered with glazed
leaves; apricots glowed among the foliage like
the rosy cheeks of a child; the boys scanned the
corpulent fig-trees with impatience, greedily
seeking the early first fruit, and in the gardens
on top of the walls, the jasmines exhaled their
suave fragrance, and the magnolias, like incen-
sories of ivory, scattered their perfume in the

burning atmosphere, impregnated with the odour of ripe fruit.

The gleaming sickles were shearing the fields, felling low the golden heads of wheat, the heavy ears of grain, which oppressed with superabundance of life, were bending toward the ground, their slender stalks doubling beneath them.

On the threshing-floor the straw was mounting up, forming hills of gold which reflected the light of the sun; the wheat was fanned amid the whirling clouds of dust, and in the fields whose tops were lopped off, along the stubble, the sparrows hopped about, seeking the forgotten grains.

Every one was happy, all worked joyfolly. The carts creaked on all the roads, bands of boys ran over the fields, or gambled on the threshing-floors, thinking of the cakes of new wheat, of the life of abundance and satisfaction which began in the farm-house upon the filling of the lofts; even the old nags seemed to look on with happy eyes, and to walk with more alacrity, as though stimulated by the odour of the mounds of straw which, like rivers of gold, would slip through their cribs during the course of the year.

The money, hoarded in the bedrooms during the winter, hidden away in the chest or in the depth of a stocking, began to circulate through the *vega.* Toward the close of the day, the taverns began to fill with men, reddened and bronzed by the sun, their rough shirts soaked with sweat, who talked about the harvest and the payment of Saint John, the half-year's rent which they had to pay over to the masters of the land.

The abundance had also brought happiness to the farm-house of Batiste. The crops had made them forget the little "Abbot." Only the mother, with sudden tears and some profound sighs, revealed the fleeting remembrance of the little one.

It was the wheat, the full sacks which Batiste and his son carried up to the granary, and which made the floor tremble, and the whole house shake as they fell from their shoulders, that interested all the family.

The good season began. Their good fortune now was as extreme as their past misfortune. The days slipped by in saintly calm and much work, but without the slightest incident to disturb the monotony of a laborious existence.

The affection which all the neighbours had shown at the burial of the little one had somewhat cooled down. As the remembrance of this misfortune became deadened, the people seemed to repent of the spontaneous impulse of tenderness and recalled once more the catastrophe of old Barret and the arrival of the intruders.

But the peace spontaneously made before the white casket of the little one was not disturbed by this. Somewhat cold and suspicious, yes; but all exchanged salutations with the family; the sons were able to go through the plain without being annoyed, and even Pimentó when he met Batiste, would nod his head in a friendly manner, mumbling something which was like an answer to his salutation.

In short, those who did not like them, left them alone, which was all that they could desire.

And in the interior of the farm-house, what abundance . . . what tranquillity! Batiste was surprised at the harvest. The lands, rested, untouched by cultivation for a long time, seemed to have sent forth at one time all the life accumulated in their depths after ten years of repose. The grain was heavy and abundant. According to the news which circulated through the plain, it was going to command a good price, and what was better (Batiste smiled on thinking of this), he did not need to pay out the profit as rent, for

he was exempt for two years. He had paid
well for this advantage by many months of
alarm and struggle and by the death of poor
Pascualet.

The prosperity of the family seemed to be reflected in the farm-house, clean and brilliant as
never before. Seen at a distance, it stood out
from the neighbouring houses, as though revealing that it had in it more prosperity and peace.
Nobody would have recognized in it the tragic
house of old Barret.

The red bricks of the pavement in front of the
door shone, polished by the daily rubbings; the
flower-beds of sweet-basil and morning-glories
and the bind-weeds formed pavilions of green,
on top of which, outlined against the sky, stood
out the sharp, triangular pediment of the farm-
house, of immaculate whiteness; within might be
seen the fluttering of the white curtains which
covered the windows of the bedrooms, the shelves
with piles of plates and concave platters leaning
against the wall, showing big fantastic birds,
and flowers like tomatoes painted on the background, and on the pitcher-shelf, which looked
like an altar of glazed tile, there appeared, like
divinities against thirst, the fat enamelled pitch-

ers, and the jars of china and greenish glass, hanging from nails in a row.

The ancient and ill-treated furniture, which was a continuous reminder of the old wanderings and fleeing from misery, began to disappear, leaving space for others, which the diligent Teresa bought on her trips to the city. The money from the harvest was invested in repairing the breaches in the furniture of the farm-house made by the months of waiting.

The family smiled at times, recalling the threatening words of Pimentó. This wheat, which according to the bully, nobody should reap, began to fatten all the family. Roseta had two more skirts, and Batistet and the little ones strutted about on Sundays, dressed anew from head to foot.

While crossing the plain during the sunniest hours, when the atmosphere burned, and the flies and bees buzzed heavily, one felt a sensation of comfort before this farm-house, which was so fresh and clean. The corral through its walls of mud and stakes, revealed the life which it enclosed. The hens clucked, the cock crowed, the rabbits leaped forth from the burrows of a great pile of new kindling; the ducks, watched

by the two little sons of Teresa, swam upon the
nearby canal, and the flocks of chickens ran
over the stubble, peeping without ceasing, moving their little rosy bodies, scarcely covered with
fine down.

To say nothing of the fact that Teresa shut
herself up in her bedroom more than once, and
opening a drawer of the dresser, untied handkerchief after handkerchief, in order to go into
ecstasies before a little heap of silver coins, the
first money which her husband had been able to
make the fields yield. This was just a beginning, and if times should be good, more and
more money would be added to this, and who
knows if when the time came these savings might
not free the little ones from military service.

The concentrated and silent joy of the mother
was noted also in Batiste.

One should have seen him on a Sunday afternoon, smoking a cuarto-stogie in honour of the
festival, passing before the house, and watching
his fields lovingly. Two days before, he had
planted corn and beans in them, as almost all of
his neighbours had, since the earth must not be
allowed to remain idle.

He could hardly manage with the two fields

which he had broken up and cultivated. But like old Barret, he felt the intoxication of the land; he wished to take in more and more with his labour, and though it was somewhat late, he planned on the following day to break up that part of the uncultivated earth which remained behind the farm-house, and plant melons there, an unsurpassed crop, from which his wife might make a very good profit, taking them as others did to the market at Valencia.

He should thank God for finally permitting him to live at peace in this paradise. What lands were these of the plain! According to history, even the Moorish dogs had wept upon being ejected from them.

The reaping had cleared the countryside, bringing low the masses of wheat variegated with poppies which shut in the view on all sides like ramparts of gold; now the plain seemed to be much larger, infinite; it stretched out and out until the large patches of red earth, cut up by paths and canals, disappeared from view.

Over all the plain the Sunday holiday was rigorously observed, and as there was a recent harvest, and not a little money, nobody thought of violating the rule. There was not a single

man to be seen working in the fields, nor a horse
upon the roads. The old women passed over
the paths with the snowy mantle over their eyes,
and their little chair upon their arm, as if the
bells which were ringing in the distance, very
far away, over the tiled roofs of the village,
were calling them; along a cross-road, a numerous group of children were screaming, pursuing
one another; over the green of the sloping-banks
stood out the red trousers of some soldiers who
were taking advantage of the holiday, to spend
an hour in their homes; there sounded in the distance, like the sharp ripping of cloth, the reports
of shot-guns fired at flocks of swallows which
were wheeling about from one side to the other in
a capricious quadrille, emitting mellow whistles,
so high it seemed they would graze their wings
against the crystal blue of the sky; over the
canals buzzed clouds of mosquitoes, almost invisible; and in a green farm-house, under the
old vine-arbour, there stirred about, in a kaleido-
scopic maze of colours, flowered skirts and
showy handkerchiefs, and the guitars sounded
with a dreamy rhythm, lulling to sleep at last
the cornet which was shrieking, pouring forth to
every end of the plain, as it slept beneath the

sun, the Moorish sounds of the *jota*, the Valencian dance.

This tranquil landscape was the idealization of laborious and happy Arcadia. There could be no evil people here. Upon awakening, Batiste stretched himself with a pleasurable feeling of laziness, yielding to the tranquil comfort with which the atmosphere seemed to be impregnated. Roseta had gone away with the little ones to a dance at a farm-house: his wife was taking her siesta, and he was walking back and forth from his house to the road over the bit of uncultivated land which served as an entrance for vehicles.

Standing on the little bridge, he answered the salutations of the neighbours, who passed by laughing, as if they were going to witness a very funny spectacle.

They were going to Copa's tavern to see at close range the famous contest between Pimentó and the two brothers, Terrerola, two bad characters like the husband of Pepeta, who also had sworn hatred to work, and passed the whole day in the tavern. Among them sprung up no end of rivalry and bets, especially when a time like this arrived, when the gatherings at the establishment swelled. The three bullies outdid one another in brutality, each one anxious to acquire more renown than the others.

Batiste had heard of this bet, which was drawing people to the famous tavern as though it were a public festivity.

The proposition was to see who could remain seated longest playing at cards, and drinking nothing but brandy.

They started Friday evening, and on Sunday afternoon, the three were still in their little rope-chairs, playing the hundredth game of cards, with the jug of *aguardiente* on the little table before them, leaving the cards only to swallow the savoury blood-pudding which gave great fame to Copa, because he knew so well how to preserve it in oil.

And the news, spreading itself throughout all the plain, made all the people come in a procession from a league roundabout. The three bullies were not alone for a moment. They had their supporters, who assumed the duty of occupying the fourth place in the game, and upon the coming of the night, when the mass of spectators retired to their farms, they remained there, watching them play in the light of the candle dangling from a black poplar-tree, for Copa was

an impatient fellow, incapable of putting up with
the tiresome wager, and so when the hour for
sleep arrived, he would close the door, and after
renewing their supply of brandy leave the players in the little square.

Many feigned indignation at the brutal contest, but at bottom they all felt satisfaction in
having such men for neighbours. Such men
were reared by the *huerta!* The brandy passed
through their bodies as if it were water.

All the neighbourhood seemed to have an eye
fixed upon the tavern, spreading the news about
the course of the bet with prodigious celerity.
Two pitchers had already been drunk, and no
effect at all. Then three . . . and still they
were steady. Copa kept account of the drinking. And the people, according to their prefer-
ence, bet for one or the other of the three con-
testants.

This event, which for two days had stirred up
so much interest in the *vega*, and did not yet seem
to have any end, had reached the ears of Batiste.
He, a sober man, incapable of drinking without
feeling nauseated and having a headache, could
not avoid feeling a certain astonishment, bor-
dering on admiration, for these brutes whose

stomachs, it seemed to him, must be lined with tin-plate. It would be a spectacle worth seeing.

And with a look of envy, his eyes followed those who were going toward the tavern. Why should he not go also? He had never entered the house of Copa, in other times the den of his enemies: but now the extraordinary nature of the event justified his presence . . . and, the devil! after so much work and such a good harvest, an honest man could allow himself a little self-indulgence.

And crying out to his sleeping wife to tell her where he was going, he set out on the road toward the tavern.

The mass of people which filled the little plaza in front of the house of Copa were like a swarm of human ants. All the men of the neighbourhood were there without any coats or waistcoats, with corduroy trousers, bulging black sash and a handkerchief wound around their heads in the form of a mitre. The old people were leaning upon their heavy staffs of yellow Lira-wood, with black arabesque work; the young people with shirt-sleeves rolled up, displayed sinewy and ruddy arms, and as though in contrast moved slender wands of ash between their thick, calloused fingers. The tall black poplars which surrounded the tavern gave shade to the animated groups.

Batiste noticed attentively for the first time the famous tavern with its white walls, its painted blue windows, and its hinges inset with showy tiles of Manises.

It had two doors. One was to the wine-cellar. Through the open doors could be seen two rows of enormous casks, which reached up to the ceiling, heaps of empty and wrinkled skin-sacks, large funnels and enormous measures tinged red by the continuous flow of liquid; there at the back of the room stood the heavy cart which went to the very ends of the province to deliver purchases of wine. This dark and damp room exhaled the fumes of alcohol, the perfume of grape-juice which so intoxicated the sense of smell and disturbed the sight that one had the feeling that both earth and air would soon be drenched with wine.

Here were the treasures of Copa, which were spoken of with unction and respect by all the drunkards of the *huerta*. He alone knew the secret of the casks; his vision, penetrating the old staves, estimated the quality of the red liquid which they contained; he was the high priest of this temple of alcohol; when he wished to treat some one, he would draw forth a glass in which sparkled liquid the colour of topaz, and which was topped by a rainbow-hued crown of brilliants, as piously as though he held the monstrance in his hands.

The other door was that of the tavern itself, which was open from an hour before daybreak until ten at night; through this the light of the oil-lamp which hung above the counter cast over the black road a large and luminous square.

The walls and wainscots were of red, glazed bricks to the height of a man, and were bordered by a row of flowered tiles. From there up to the ceiling, the wall was dedicated to the sublime art of the painter, for Copa, although he seemed to be a coarse man, whose only thought was to have his cash drawer full at night, was a true Mæcenas. He had brought a painter from the city, and kept him there more than a week, and this caprice of the great protector of the arts had cost him, as he himself declared, some five dollars, more or less.

It was really true that one could not shift his gaze about without meeting with some masterful

work of art, whose loud colours seemed to glad-
den the customers and stimulate them to drink.
Blue trees over purple fields, yellow horizons,
houses larger than trees, and people larger than
houses; hunters with shot-guns which looked like
brooms, and Andalusian gallants with blunder-
busses thrown over their legs, and mounted upon
spirited steeds which had all the appearance of
gigantic rats. A prodigy of originality which
filled the drinkers with enthusiasm! And over
the doors of the rooms, the artist, referring dis-
creetly to the establishment, had painted astonishing paintings of edible delicacies; pomegran-
ates like open hearts, and bleeding melons which
looked like enormous pimientoes, and balls of
red worsted which were supposed to represent
peaches.

Many maintained that the importance of the
house over the other taverns of the *huerta* was
due to such astonishing adornment, and Copa
cursed the flies which dimmed such beauty.

Close to this door was the counter, grimy and
sticky: behind it the three rows of little casks,
crowned with battlements of bottles, all the di-
versified and innumerable liquors of the establishment. From the beams, like grotesque

babies, hung sheets of long sausages and black-
puddings, clusters of peppers as red and pointed
as devils' fingers; and relieving the monotony
of the scene, some red hams and majestic
bunches of pork-sausage. The free-lunch for
delicate palates was kept in a closet of turbid
glass close to the counter. There were the *es-
trellas de pastaflora,*[1] the raisin-cakes, the sugar-
frosted rolls, the *magdalenas*[2] all of a certain
dark tinge and with suspicious spots which
showed old age; the cheese of Murviedo, tender
and fresh, pieces like soft white loaves still
dripping whey.

Also the tavern-keeper counted on his larder,
where in monumental tins were the green split
olives and the black-puddings of onion preserved
in oil, which had the greatest sale.

At the back of the tavern opened the door of
the yard, vast and spacious with its half dozen
fireplaces to cook the *paellas*[3]; its white pillars
propping up an old wall-vine, which gave shade
to the large enclosure; and piled along one side
of the wall, stools and small zinc tables of such

[1] Star-cakes—a local provincial dainty.
[2] Long, boat-shaped rolls.
[3] A Valencian dish of rice, meat and vegetables.

prodigious quantity that Copa seemed to have foreseen the invasion of his house by the whole population of the plain.

Batiste, scanning the tavern, perceived the owner, a big man whose breast was bare, but whose cap with ear-laps was drawn down even in midsummer over his face, which was enormous, chubby-cheeked and livid. He was the first customer of his establishment: he would never lie down satisfied if he had not drunk a half-pitcher of wine during his three meals.

On this account, doubtless, this bet which stirred up the entire plain as it spread abroad, scarcely took his attention.

His counter was the watch-tower from which, as an expert critic, he watched the drunkenness of his customers. And in order that no outsider should assume the rôle of bully in his house, he always put his hand before speaking upon a club which he kept under the counter, a species of ace of clubs, the sight of which made Pimentó and all the bullies of the neighbourhood tremble. In his house there was no trouble. If they were going to kill each other, out into the road! And when claspknives began to be opened and raised aloft on Sunday nights, Copa, without speaking

a word, nor losing his composure, would rush
in between the combatants, seize the bravest by
the arm, carry him through space to the door and
put him out upon the very highroad; then barring the door, he would calmly begin to count
the money in the drawer before going to bed,
while blows and the tumult of the renewed quarrel resounded outside. It was all just a matter of closing the tavern an hour early, but within
it, there would never need to be a judge while he
should be behind the counter.

Batiste, after glancing furtively from the door
to the saloonkeeper, who, aided by his wife and
a servant, waited on the customers, returned to
the little plaza, and joined a group of old people, who were discussing which of the three supporters of the bet seemed most serene.

Many farmers, tired of admiring the three
bullies, were playing cards on their own account,
or lunched, forming a group around the little
tables. The jug circulated, pouring forth a red
stream which emitted a faint *glu-glu* as it gushed
into the open mouths. Some gave others hand-
fuls of peanuts and lupines. The maids of the
tavern served in hollow plates from Manises the
dark and oily black-puddings, the fresh cheese

and the split olives in their broth, on whose surface floated fragrant herbs; and on the little
tables appeared the new wheat bread, the rolls
of ruddy crust, inside of which the dark and
succulent substance of the thick flour of the
huerta was visible. All these people, eating,
drinking, and gesticulating, raised such a buzzing that one would have thought the little *plaza*
occupied by a colossal wasp's nest. In the atmosphere floated the vapours of alcohol, the
suffocating fumes of olive-oil, the penetrating
odour of must, mingled with the fresh perfume
of the neighbouring fields.

Batiste drew near the large group which surrounded those involved in the wager.

At first he did not see anything; but gradually,
pushed ahead by the curiosity of those who were
behind him, he opened a space between the
sweaty and compressed bodies, until he found
himself in the first row. Some spectators were
seated on the floor, with their chin supported on
both hands, their nose over the edge of the little
table, and their eyes fixed upon the players, as
though they did not wish to lose one detail of the
famous event. Here it was that the odour of
alcohol proved to be most intolerable. The

breath and the clothing of all the people seemed impregnated with it.

Batiste looked at Pimentó and his opponents seated upon stools of strong carob-wood, with the cards before their eyes, the jar of brandy within easy reach, and on the zinc the little heap of corn which was equivalent to chips for the game. And at each play, one of the three grasped the jar, drank deliberately, then passed it on to his companions, who took a long draft with no less ceremony.

The onlookers nearest by looked at the cards over their shoulders in order to be sure they were well played. But the heads of the players were as steady as if they had drunk nothing more than water: no one became careless or made a poor play.

And the game continued, although those in the wager never ceased to talk with their friends, or to joke over the outcome of the contest.

Pimentó, upon seeing Batiste, mumbled a "Hello!" which he intended for a salutation, and returned to his cards.

Unmoved outwardly he might be; but his eyes were red; a bluish unsteady spark, similar to the flame of alcohol, glowed in their pupils, and his face at times took on a dull pallor. The others were no better; but they laughed and joked among themselves: the onlookers, as though infected by this madness, passed from hand to hand the jug which they paid for in shares, and there was a regular inundation of brandy which, overflowing the tavern, descended like a wave of fire into the stomachs of all.

Even Batise, urged by the others of the group, had to drink. He did not like it, but a man ought to try everything; and he began to hearten himself with the same reflections which had brought him to the tavern. When a man has worked and has his harvest in the granary, he can well afford to permit himself his bit of folly.

He felt a warmth in his stomach, and a delicious confusion in his head: he began to grow accustomed to the atmosphere of the tavern, and found the contest more and more entertaining.

Even Pimentó seemed to him to be a notable man . . . after a fashion.

They had ended the game with a score of . . . (nobody knew how much) and they were now discussing the approaching supper with their friends. One of the Terrerolas was losing ground visibly. The two days of brandy-drink-

ing without food, the two nights passed in a haze,
began to affect him in spite of himself. He
closed his eyes and let his head fall back heavily
upon his brother, who revived him with tremen-
dous blows on the sides secretly given under the
table.

Pimentó smiled craftily. He already had one
of them down. And he discussed the supper
with his admirers. It ought to be sumptuous
without regard for expense: in any event, he did
not have to pay for it. A meal which would be
a worthy climax to the exploit, for on that
same night, the bet would surely be ended.

And like a glorious trumpet announcing be-
forehand Pimentó's triumph, the snores of Terrerola the younger began to be heard; he had
collapsed face downward over the table, and was
almost on the point of falling from the stool, as
if all the brandy which had gone into his stomach were by the law of gravity seeking the floor.

His brother spoke of arousing him with slaps,
but Pimentó intervened good-naturedly, like a
magnanimous conqueror. They would awaken
him at the supper-hour. And pretending to give
but little importance to the contest and to his
own prowess, he spoke of his lack of appetite as

of a great misfortune, after having passed two days in this place eating and drinking brutally.

A friend ran to the tavern to carry over a long string of red pepper-pods. This would bring his appetite back to him. The jest provoked great laughter; and Pimentó, in order to amaze his admirers the more, offered the infernal titbit to Terrerola, who still remained firm, and he, on his part, began to devour it with the same indifference as though it were bread.

A murmur of admiration ran through the group. For each pod which was eaten by the other, the husband of Pepeta gulped down three, and thus made an end of the string, a regular rosary of red demons. The brute must have an iron-plate stomach!

And he went on, just as firm, just as impassive, though growing continually paler and with eyes red and swollen, asking if Copa had killed a pair of chickens for the supper, and giving instructions about the manner of cooking them.

Batiste gazed at this with amazement and vaguely felt a desire to go away. The afternoon began to wane; in the little square the sound of voices was rising, the tumult of every Sunday evening beginning, and Pimentó gazed at him too

often, with his strange and troubling eyes, the
eyes of a habitual drinker. But without knowing why, he remained here, as though the attrac-
tion of this spectacle, so novel to him, were
stronger than his will.

The friends of the bully jested with him on
seeing that he was draining the jar after the red
pepper-pods, without even heeding whether his
weary rival was imitating him. He ought not to
drink so much: he would lose, and he would not
have the money to pay. He was not as rich
now as he had been in other years, when the
masters of the lands had agreed not to charge
him any rent.

An imprudent fellow said this without realizing what he was saying, and it produced a painful silence, as in the bedroom of an invalid, when
the injured part has been laid bare.

To speak of rents and of payments in this
place, when brandy had been drunk by pitchers-
ful both by actors and spectators!

Batiste received a disagreeable impression.
It seemed to him that suddenly there passed
through the atmosphere something hostile,
threatening; without any great urging, he would
have started to run; but he remained, feeling

that all were looking fixedly at him. He feared
that he would be held by insults if he fled before
he was attacked; and with the hope of being un-
molested, he remained motionless, overcome by
a feeling which was not fear, but something more
than prudence.

These people, whom Pimentó filled with admiration, made him repeat the method which he
had made use of, all these years, to avoid paying
his rent to the masters of the lands, and greeted
it with loud bursts of laughter, and tremors of
malignant joy, like slaves who rejoice at the
misfortunes of a master.

The bully modestly related his glorious
achievements. Every year at Christmas and St.
John's Day, he had set out on the road to Valencia at full speed to see his landlord. Others
carried a fine brace of chickens, a basket of
cakes or fruits as a means to persuade the masters to accept incomplete payment, and would
weep and promise to complete the sum before
long. He alone carried words and not many of
them.

The mistress, a large, imposing woman, received him in the dining-room. The daughters,
proud young ladies, all dressed up with bows of

ribbons and bright colours, came and went nearby.

Doña Manuela turned to the memorandum book, to look up the half-years that Pimentó was behind. He came to pay, eh? . . . And the crafty rogue, upon hearing the question of the lady of the "Hay-Lofts" always answered the same. No, señora, he could not pay because he hadn't a copper. He was not ignorant of the fact that by this he was proving himself a scamp. His grandfather, who was a man of great wisdom, had told him so. "For whom were chains forged? For men. Do you pay? You are an honest man. Do you not pay? You are a rogue." And following this short discourse on philosophy, he had recourse to the second argument. He drew forth a black stogie and a pocket-knife from his sash, and began to pick tobacco in order to roll a cigarette.

The sight of the weapon sent chills through the lady, made her nervous; and for this very reason the crafty fellow cut the tobacco slowly and was deliberate about putting it away. Always repeating the same arguments of the grandfather, in order to explain his tardiness about the payment.

The children with the little bows of ribbon
called him "the man of the chains"; the mamma
felt uneasy in the presence of this rough fellow
of black reputation, who smelt vilely of wine,
and gesticulated with the knife as he talked; and
convinced that nothing could be gotten from him,
she told him that he might go; but he felt a deep
joy in being troublesome, and tried to prolong
the interview.   They even went so far as to say
that if he could not pay anything, he could even
spare them his visits and not appear there further; they would forget that they had those lands.
Ah, no, señora.   Pimentó fulfilled his obliga-
tions punctually, and as a tenant, he should visit
his landlord at Christmas and San Juan, in order
to show that though he was not paying, he remained nevertheless their very humble servant.

And there he would go, twice a year, smelling
of wine, and stain the floor with his sandals, clay
covered, and repeat that chains were made for
men, making sabre-thrusts the while with his
knife.   It was the vengeance of the slave, the
bitter pleasure of the mendicant who appears in
the midst of a feast of rich men, with his foul
tatters.

All the farmers laughed, commenting on the conduct of Pimentó with his landlord.

And the bully justified his conduct with arguments. Why should he pay? Come now, why? His grandfather had cultivated his lands before him; at his father's death they had been divided among the brothers at their pleasure, following the custom of the *huerta*, and without consulting the landlord in any way. They were the ones who had worked them; they had made them produce, they had worn away their lives upon their fields.

Pimentó, speaking with vehemence of his work, showed such shamelessness that some smiled. . . . Good: he was not working much now, because he was shrewd and had recognized the farce of living. But at one time he had worked, and this was enough to make the lands more justly his own than they were of that big, fat woman of Valencia. When she would come to work them; when she would take the plough with all its weight, and the two little girls with the bows yoked together would draw it after them, then she would legitimately be the mistress.

The coarse jokes of the bully made the peo-

ple roar with laughter. The bad flavour of the
payment of St. John remained with them and
they took much pleasure in seeing their masters
treated so cruelly. Ah! The joke about the
plough was very funny; and each one imagined
that he could see the master, the stout and timid
landlord, or the señora, old and proud, hitched
up to the ploughshare pulling and pulling, while
they, the farmers, those under the heel, were
cracking the whip.

And all winked at each other, laughed and
clapped their hands, in order to express their
approbation. Oh! It was very comfortable in
the house of Copa listening to Pimentó. What
ideas the man had!

But the husband of Pepeta became gloomy,
and many noticed that often he would cast a side-
long look about him, that look of murder which
was long known in the tavern to be a certain
sign of immediate aggression. His voice became thick, as if all the alcohol which was swell-
ing his stomach had ascended like a hot wave
and burned his throat.

They might laugh until they burst, but their
laughs would be the last. Already the *huerta*
was not the same as it had been for ten years.

The masters, who had been timid rabbits, had again become unruly wolves. They were showing their teeth again. Even his mistress had taken liberties with him. With him. who was the terror of all the landowners of the *huerta!* During his visit last St. John's day she had laughed at his saying about the chains, and even at the knife, announcing to him that he might prepare either to leave the lands or pay his rent, not forgetting the back payments either.

And why had they turned in such a manner? Because already they no longer feared them. . . . And why did they not fear them? Christ! Because now the fields of old Barret were no longer abandoned and uncultivated, a phantom of desolation to awe the landlords and make them sweet and reasonable. So the charm had been broken. Since a half-starved thief had succeeded in imposing himself upon them, the landlords had laughed, and wishing to take revenge for ten years of enforced meekness, had grown worse than the infamous Don Salvador.

"True . . . it is true," said all the group, supporting the arguments of Pimentó, with furious nods.

All confessed that their landlords had changed

as they recalled the details of their last interview; the threats of ejection, the refusal to accept the incomplete payments, the ironical way
in which they had spoken of the lands of old
Barret, cultivated again in spite of the hatred of
all the *huerta*.   And now, all at once, after the
sweet laziness of ten years of triumph, with the
reins on their shoulders and the master at their
feet, had come the cruel pull, the return to other
times, the finding of the bread bitter and the wine
more sour, thinking of the accursed half-year,
and all on account of an outsider, a lousy fellow
who had not even been born in the *huerta*, and
who had hung himself upon them to interfere in
their business and make life harder for them.
And should this rogue still live?   Did the *huerta*
not have any men?

Good-bye, new friendships, respect born by
the side of the coffin of a poor child!   All the
consideration created by misfortune went tumbling down like a stock of playing-cards, vanish-
ing like a nebulous cloud, and the old hatred re-
appeared at a single bound—the solidarity of
all the *huerta,* which in combating the intruder
was defending its very life.

And at what a moment the general animosity

arose! The eyes fixed upon him burned with the fire of hatred; heads muddled with alcohol seemed to feel a horrible itching for murder; instinctively they all started toward Batiste, who felt himself pushed about from all sides as if the circle were tightening in order to devour him.

He repented now of having remained. He felt no fear, but he cursed the hour in which the idea of going to the tavern occurred to him—an alien place which seemed to rob him of his strength, that self-possession which animated him when he felt the earth beneath his feet—the earth which he had cultivated at the cost of so much sacrifice, and in whose defence he was ready to lose his very life.

Pimentó, as he gave way to his anger, felt all the brandy he had drunk during the past two days fall suddenly like a heavy blow upon his brain. He had lost the serenity of an unshakable drunkard; he arose staggering, and it was necessary for him to make an effort to sustain himself upon his legs. His eyes were inflamed as though they were dripping blood; his voice was laboured as though the alcohol and anger were drawing it back and not letting it come forth.

"Go," he said imperiously to Batiste, threat-
eningly, extending a hand, till it almost touched
his face. "Go, or I will kill you!"

Go! . . . It was this that Batiste desired; he
grew paler and paler, repenting more and more
that he was here. But he well divined the significance of that imperious "Go!" of the bully,
supported by signs of approval on the part of all
the others.

They did not demand that he should leave the
tavern, ridding them of his odious presence; they
were ordering him with threats of death to abandon the fields, which were like the blood of his
body; to give up for ever the farm-house where
his little one had died, and in which every corner
bore a record of the struggles and the joys of the
family in their battle with poverty. And swiftly
he had a vision of himself and all his furniture
piled on the cart, wandering over the roads, in
search of the unknown, in order to create another
existence: carrying along with them like a
gloomy companion, that ugly phantom of famine
which would be ever following at their heels. . . .

No! He shunned quarrels, but let them not
put a finger on his children's bread!

Now he felt no disquietude. The image of

his family, hungry and without a hearth, enraged him; he even felt a desire to attack all
these people who demanded of him such a monstrous thing.

"Will you go? Will you go?" asked Pimentó, ever darker and more threatening.

No: he would not go. He said it with his
head, with his smile of scorn, with his firm
glance and the challenging look which he fixed
upon the group.

"Scoundrel!" roared the bully; and his hand
fell upon the face of Batiste, giving it a terrible
resounding slap.

As though stirred by this aggression, all the
group rushed upon the odious intruder, but
above the line of heads a muscular arm arose,
grasping a rush-grass stool, the same perhaps
upon which Pimentó had been seated.

For the strong Batiste it was a terrible weapon,
this seat of strong cross-pieces, with heavy legs
of carob-wood, its corners polished by usage.

The little table and the jars of brandy rolled
away, the people backed instinctively, terrified
by the gesture of this man, always so peaceful,
who seemed now a giant in his madness. But
before any one could recede a step, Plaf! a noise

resounded like a bursting kettle, and Pimentó, his head broken, fell to the ground.

In the *plaza*, it produced an indescribable confusion.

Copa, who from his lair seemed to pay attention to nothing, and was the first to scent a quarrel, no sooner saw the stool in the air than he drew out the "ace of clubs" which was under the counter, and with a few quick blows, in a jiffy cleared the tavern of its customers and immediately closed the door in accordance with his usual salutary custom.

The people remained outside, running around the little square; the tables rolled about. Sticks and clubs were brandished in the air, each one placing himself on guard against his neighbour, ready for whatever might come; and in the meantime Batiste, the cause of all the trouble, stood motionless, with hanging arms, grasping the stool now stained with spots of blood, terrified by what had just occurred.

Pimentó, face downward on the ground, uttered groans which sounded like snarls, as the blood gushed forth from his broken head.

Terrerola, the elder, with the fraternal feeling of one drunkard for another ran to the aid of his rival, looking with hostility at Batiste. He insulted him, looking in his sash for a weapon with which to wound him.

The most peaceful fled away through the paths, looking back with morbid curiosity, and the others remained motionless, on the defensive, each one capable of dispatching his neighbour, without knowing why, but not one wishing to be the first aggressor. The clubs remained raised aloft, the clasp knives gleamed in the group, but no one approached Batiste, who slowly backed away, still holding the bloodstained tabouret aloft.

Thus he left the little plaza, ever looking with challenging eyes at the group which surrounded the fallen Pimentó, all brave fellows but evidently intimidated by this man's strength.

Upon finding himself on the road, at some distance from the tavern, he began to run, and drawing near his farm-house, he dropped the heavy stool in a canal, looking with horror at the blackish stain of the dry blood upon the water.

X

BATISTE lost all hope of living peacefully on his land.

The entire *huerta* once more arose against him. Again he had to isolate himself in his farm-house, to live in perpetual solitude like one cursed by a plague, or like some caged wild-beast, at whom every one shook his fist from afar.

His wife told him on the following day how the wounded bully was conducted to his house. He himself, from his home, had heard the shouts and the threats of the people, who had solicitously accompanied the wounded Pimentó. . . . It was a real manifestation. The women, already aware of what had happened through the marvellous rapidity with which news spreads over the *huerta,* ran out on the road to see Pepeta's brave husband at close range, and to express compassion for him as for some hero sacrificed for the good of others.

The same ones who had spoken insultingly of

him some hours before, scandalized by his wager of drunkenness, now pitied him, inquired whether he was seriously hurt, and clamoured for revenge against that starving pauper, that thief, who not content with taking possession of that which was not his, tried to win respect by terror, and by attacking good men.

Pimentó was magnificent. He suffered great pain, and went about supported by his friends with his head bandaged, transformed into an *eccehomo,* as the indignant gossips declared; but he made an effort to smile, and answered every incitement to revenge with an arrogant gesture, declaring that he took the castigation of the enemy upon himself.

Batiste did not doubt that these people would seek vengeance. He was familiar with the usual methods of the *huerta.* The courts of the city were not made for this land; prison was a small matter when a question of satisfying a grudge was concerned. Why should a man make use of a judge or a civil guard, if he had a good eye and a shotgun in his house? The affairs of men should be settled by the men themselves.

And as all the *huerta* thought thus, vainly on the day following the quarrel did two guards with

enamelled tricorns pass and repass over the paths
leading from Copa's tavern to the farm-house of
Pimentó, making sly inquiries of the people who
were in the fields. No one had seen anybody;
no one knew anything. Pimentó related with
brutal bursts of laughter how he had broken his
own head coming home from the tavern, declaring it to be the consequence of his bet; the brandy
had made him stagger, and strike his head
against the trees on the road. So the rural police
had to turn back to their little barracks at Alboraya without any clear information concerning
the vague rumours of quarrel and bloodshed
which had reached them.

This magnanimity of the victim and his
friends alarmed Batiste, who made up his mind
to live perpetually on the defensive.

The family, shrinking from contact with the
huerta, withdrew within the house as a timid snail
withdraws within its shell.

The little ones did not even go to school.
Roseta stopped going to the factory, and Batistet
did not go a pace away from the fields. Only
the father went out, showing himself as calm and
confident about his security as he was careful and
prudent for the others.

But he made no trips to the city without carrying the shotgun with him, which he left with a friend in the suburbs. He literally lived with his weapon. The most modern thing in his house, it was always clean, shining and cared for with that affection which the Valencian farmer, like the Barbary tribesman, bestows upon his gun.

Teresa was as sad as she had been upon the death of the little one. Every time that she saw her husband cleaning the double-barrelled shotgun, changing the cartridges, or making the trigger play up and down to be sure it would work smoothly, there arose in her mind the image of the prison, the terrible tale of old Barret; she saw blood and cursed the hour in which they had thought of settling upon these accursed lands. And then came the hours of fear on account of the absence of her husband, those long afternoons spent awaiting the man who did not return, going out to the door of the farm-house to explore the road, trembling each time that there sounded from the distance some report from the hunters of sparrows, fearing that it was the beginning of a tragedy, the shot which shattered the head of the father of the family or which would take him to prison. And when Batiste finally appeared, the little ones would shout with joy, Teresa would smile, wiping her eyes, the daughter would run out to embrace her father, and even the dog leaped close to him, sniffing restlessly, as though he scented about his person the danger which he had just encountered.

And Batiste, serene and firm, but without arro-gance, laughed at his family's anxiety, and be-came bolder and bolder as the famous quarrel receded into the past.

He considered himself secure. As long as he carried "the bird with the two voices," as he called his shotgun, he could calmly walk through-out all the *huerta*. When he went out in such good company, his enemies pretended not to know him. At times he had even seen Pimentó from a distance, walking through the *huerta*, ex-hibiting like a flag of vengeance his bandaged head, but the bully, in spite of his recovery from the blow had fled, fearing the encounter perhaps even more than Batiste.

All were watching him from the corner of their eye, but he never heard from the fields adjoin-ing the road a single word of insult. They shrugged their shoulders with scorn, bent over the earth, and worked feverishly until he was lost from sight.

The only person who spoke to him was old Tomba, the crazy shepherd, who recognized him despite his sightless eyes, as though he could scent the atmosphere of calamity around Batiste.   And it was ever the same. . . . Was he not going to abandon the accursed lands?

"You are making a mistake, my son; they will bring you misfortune."

Batiste received the refrain of the old man with a smile.

Grown familiar with peril, he had never feared it less than he did now.   He even felt a certain secret joy in provoking it, in marching directly toward it.   His tavern exploit had changed his character, previously so peaceful and long-suffering; awakened in him a boastful brutality. He wished to show all these people that he did not fear them, that even as he had burst open Pimentó's head, so was he ready to take up arms against the whole *huerta*.   Since they had driven him to it, he would be a bully and a braggart long enough for them to respect him and allow him to live peacefully ever afterward.

And possessed of this dangerous determination, he even abandoned his lands, passing the afternoons along the roads of the *huerta* under the pretext of hunting, but in reality to exhibit his shotgun and his look of a man who has few friends.

One afternoon, while hunting swallows in the ravine of Carraixet, the darkness surprised him.

The birds seemed to be following the mazes of some capricious quadrille as they flew about restlessly, reflected in the deep and quiet pools bordered with tall rushes. This ravine, which cut across the *huerta* like a deep crack, gloomy, with stagnant water, and muddy shores, where there bobbed up and down some rotting, half-submerged canoe, presented a desolate and wild aspect. No one would have suspected that behind the slope of the high banks, farther on beyond the rushes and the cane-brake, lay the plain with its smiling atmosphere and its green vistas. Even the light of the sun seemed dismal, as it sank to the depths of the ravine, sifting through the wild vegetation and pallidly reflecting itself in the dead waters.

Batiste spent the afternoon firing at the wheeling swallows. A few cartridges still remained in his belt, and at his feet, forming a mound of blood-stained feathers, he already had two dozen birds. What a supper! How happy the family would be!

It grew dark in the deep ravine: from the pools, a fetid vapour came forth, the deadly respiration of malarial fever. The frogs croaked by the thousand, as though saluting the stars, contented at not hearing the firing which interrupted their song, and obliged them to dive head-long, disturbing the smooth crystal of the stagnant pools.

Batiste picked up his "bag" of birds, hanging them from the belt, and ascending the bank with two leaps, set out over the paths on his return trip to the farm-house.

The sky, still permeated with the faint glow of twilight, had the soft tone of violet; the stars gleamed, and over the immense *huerta* there rose the many sounds of rustic life which would soon with the arrival of night die away. Over the paths passed the girls returning from the city; and men coming from the fields, the tired horses dragging the heavy carts; and Batiste answered their "Good night," the greeting of all who passed near him, people from Alboraya, who did not know him or did not have the motives of his neighbours for hating him.

He left the village behind him, and as he drew nearer to his farm, the hostility stood out more plainly with every step. The people hissed him without any greeting.

He was in strange country, and like a soldier who prepares to fight as soon as he crosses the hostile frontier, Batiste sought in his sash for the munitions of war, two cartridges with ball and bird-shot, made by himself, and loaded his shot-gun.

The big man laughed after doing this. Who-ever tried to cut off his way would receive a good shower of lead.

He walked along without haste, calmly, as though enjoying the freshness of the spring night. But this tranquillity did not prevent him from thinking of the risk he was taking, with the ene-mies he had, in being abroad in the *huerta* at such an hour.

His keen ear, that of a countryman, seemed to perceive a sound at his shoulder. He turned about quickly, and in the pale star-light, he thought he saw a dark figure, leaping from the road with a stealthy bound and hiding behind a bank.

Batiste laid hold of his shotgun, and lifting the hammer, approached cautiously. No one. . . . Only at some distance it seemed to him that the plants were waving in the darkness, as though a body were dragging itself among them.

They were following him: some one intended to surprise him treacherously from behind. But this suspicion lasted but a short time. It might be some vagabond dog which fled upon his approach.

Well, it was certain that whatever it was, it was fleeing from him, and so there was nothing for him to do.

He went along over the dark road, walking silently like a man who knows the country in the dark, and for the sake of prudence does not wish to attract attention. As he approached the farm, he felt a certain uneasiness. This was his neighbourhood, but here also were his most tenacious enemies.

Some minutes before arriving at the farm, near the blue farm-house where the girls danced on Sundays, the road became narrow, forming various curves. At one side, a high bank was

crowned by a double row of mulberry-trees; on
the other, was a narrow canal whose sloping
shores were thickly covered with tall cane-brake.

It looked in the darkness like an Indian
thicket, a vault of bamboos bending over the
road. It was completely dark here; the mass of
cane-brake trembled in the light wind of the
night, giving forth a mournful sound; the place,
so cool and agreeable during the hours of sunlight, seemed to smell of treason.

Batiste, laughing at his uneasiness, mentally
exaggerated the danger. A magnificent place
to fire a safe shot at him. If Pimentó should
come along here, he would not scorn such a
beautiful chance.

And scarcely had he thought of this, when
there came forth from among the cane-brake a
straight and fleeting tongue of fire, a red arrow
which vanished, followed by a report; and something passed, hissing close to his ear. Some one
was firing upon him. Instinctively he stooped
down, wishing to fuse with the darkness of the
ground, so as not to present a target to the enemy.
In the same moment a new flash glowed, another report sounded, mingling with the echoes
still reverberating from the first, and Batiste

felt a tearing sensation in the left shoulder, something like the scratch of steel, scraping him superficially.

But his attention scarcely stopped at this. He felt a savage joy. Two shots . . . the enemy was disarmed.

"Christ! Now I've got you!"

He rushed out through the cane-brake, plunged, almost rolling down the slope, and entered the water up to the waist, his feet in the mud and his arms aloft, very high, in order to prevent his shotgun from getting wet, guarding like a miser the two shots until the moment should arrive when he could safely deal them out.

Before his eyes the cane-brake met, forming a close arch almost level with the water. Before him in the darkness, he heard a splashing like that of a dog fleeing down through the canal. Here was the enemy: after him!

And in the stream-bed, he entered on a mad race, plunging along groping through the shadows, leaving his sandals behind him, lost in the mud: his trousers, clinging to his body, and dragging heavily, retarded his movements: and the stiff sharp stalks of the broken cane-brake struck and scratched his face.

At one moment Batiste thought he saw some·
thing dark clinging to the cane-brake, striving to
rise above the bank.   He was attempting to run
away: he must fire. . . . His hands, which felt
the itching of murder, carried the shotgun to
his face, pulled the trigger, . . . the report
sounded, and the body fell into the canal, among
a shower of leaves and rotting cane.

At him!   At him! . . . Again, Batiste heard
the splashing of a fleeing dog: but now with more
effort, as though the fugitive, spurred on by des·
peration, were straining every effort to escape.

It was a dizzy flight, that race amid darkness,
through the cane-brake and water.   The two
kept slipping on the soft ground, unable to cling
to the brake without loosening their hold on their
guns; the water eddied about them, lashed by
their reckless haste, but Batiste, who fell several
times on his knees, thought only of reaching out
his arms, in order to keep his weapon dry and
save the shot which remained.

And thus the human hunters went on, groping
through the dismal darkness, until in a turn of
the canal, they came out to an open space, where
the banks were clear of reeds.

The eyes of Batiste, accustomed to the gloom

of the vault, saw with perfect clearness a man who, leaning on his firearm, climbed staggering out of the canal, with difficulty moving mud-clogged legs.

It was he . . . he! he as usual!

"Thief! . . . thief! you shall not escape," roared Batiste, and he discharged his second shot from the bottom of the canal, with the certainty of the marksman who is able to aim well and knows he brings down his booty.

He saw him fall heavily headlong over the bank, and climb on all-fours in order to roll into the water. Batiste wanted to catch him, but his haste was so great that it was he who, making a false step, fell full-length into the midst of the canal.

His head sunk in the mud, and he swallowed the earthy, ruddy liquid; he thought he would die, and remain buried in that miry marsh; but finally, by a powerful effort, he succeeded in standing upright, drawing his eyes blinded by the slime out of the water, then his mouth, panting as it breathed in the night air.

As soon as he recovered his sight, he looked for his enemy. He had disappeared.

He came out of the canal, dripping water and

mud, and climbed the slope at the same place where his enemy had emerged: but on reaching the top, he could not see him.

On the dry earth, however, he noticed some black stains, and touched them with his hands: they smelled of blood. Now he knew that he had not missed his aim. But, though he looked about, hoping to see his enemy's corpse, he sought in vain.

That Pimentó had a tough skin. Dripping mud and mire, he would go along dragging himself up to his own farm-house. Perhaps that vague rustle which he believed he heard in the immediate fields, as though a great reptile were dragging itself over the furrows, came from him. All the dogs were barking at him, filling the *huerta* with desperate howlings. He had heard him crawling along in the same manner a quarter of an hour before, when doubtless he was intending to kill him from behind. But on seeing himself discovered, he had fled on all-fours along the road, in order to take his stand further on in the leafy cane and to lie in ambush without any risk.

Batiste felt suddenly afraid. He was alone, in the midst of the plain, completely disarmed;

his shotgun, without cartridges, was no more now than a weak club. Pimentó couldn't return, but he had friends.

And overcome by sudden fear, he began to run, seeking as he crossed the fields the road which led to his farm.

The plain trembled with alarm. The four shots in the darkness of the evening had thrown all the neighbourhood into commotion. The dogs barked more and more furiously; the doors of the farm-houses opened, emitting black figures, who certainly did not come forth with empty hands.

With whistling and shouts of alarm, the neighbours summoned each other from a great distance. Shots at night might be signals of fire, of thieves, of who knows what? certainly nothing good. And the men sallied forth from their homes ready for anything, with the forgetfulness of self and solidarity of those who live in solitude.

Batiste, terrified by this movement, ran toward his farm, bending over, in order to pass unnoticed along the shelter of the banks or the high mounds of straw.

He already saw his home, with the open door

illumined, and in the centre of the red square, the black forms of his family.

The dog sniffed him and was the first to salute him. Teresa and Roseta gave shouts of joy.

"Batiste, is it you?"

"Father! Father!"

And all rushed toward him, toward the entrance of the farm-house, under the old vine-arbour, through whose vines the stars shone like glow-worms.

The mother, with the woman's keen ear, restless and alarmed by the tardiness of her husband, had heard from far, far off, the four shots, and her heart "had given a leap," as she expressed it. All the family had rushed toward the door, anxiously scanning the dark horizon, convinced that the reports which alarmed the plain had some connection with the father's absence.

Mad with joy upon seeing him and hearing his voice, they did not notice his mud-stained face, his unshod feet, or his clothing, dirty and dripping mire.

They drew him within. Roseta hung herself upon his neck, breathing lovingly, with her eyes still moist.

"Father! . . . Father!"

But he was not able to restrain a grimace of pain, an ay! suppressed but full of suffering. Roseta had flung her arm about his left shoulder, in the same place where he had felt the tearing of steel, and which he now felt more and more crushingly heavy.

When he entered the house, and came into the full candlelight, the woman and the children gave a cry of astonishment. They saw the blood-stained shirt. . . .

Roseta and her mother burst out crying. "Most holy queen! Sovereign mother! They have killed him!"

But Batiste, who felt the pain in his shoulder growing more and more insufferable, hushed their lamentations and ordered them with a dark gesture to see at once what had happened to him.

Roseta, who was the bravest, tore open the coarse rough shirt, leaving the shoulder uncovered. How much blood! The girl grew pale, trying not to faint; Batistet and the little ones began to weep, and Teresa continued her howlings as though her husband were in his death agony.

But the wounded man would not tolerate their lamentations and protested rudely. Less weeping: it was nothing: not serious, and the

proof of this was that he could move his arm,
although he felt, all the time, a greater weight in
his shoulder.   It was just a scratch, an abrasion,
nothing more.   He felt too strong for the wound
to be deep.   Look . . . water, cloth, lint, the
bottle of arnica which Teresa was guarding as a
miraculous remedy in her room . . . move
about quickly!   This was no time to stand gaping with open mouths.

Teresa, returning to her room, searched the
depths of her chests, tearing up linen cloths, un-
tying bandages, while the girl washed and
washed again the lips of the bleeding wound,
which was cut like a sabre-slash across the fleshy
shoulder.

The two women checked the hemorrhage as
best they could, bandaged the wound, and Batiste breathed with satisfaction, as though he were
already cured.   Worse blows than this had descended upon him in this life.

And he began to admonish the little ones to be
prudent.   Of what they had seen, not a word to
anybody.   There are subjects which it is best to
forget.   And he repeated the same to his wife,
who talked of sending word to the doctor; it
would amount to the same thing as attracting the

attention of the court. It would cure itself. His constitution was wonderful. What was important was that no one should get mixed up in what occurred down below. Who knows in what condition the other man was by this time?

While his wife was helping him to change his clothes and prepared his bed, Batiste told her all that had occurred. The good woman opened her eyes with a frightened expression, sighed, thinking of the danger encountered by her husband, and cast anxious glances at the closed door of the farm-house, as if the rural police were about to enter through it.

Batistet, meanwhile, with precocious prudence, picked up the gun, and dried it in the candlelight, striving to wipe away from it all signs of recent usage, of that which had occurred.

The night was a bad one for all the family; Batiste was delirious; he had a fever, and tossed about furiously as if he still were running along the bed of the canal, pursuing the man. He terrified the little ones with his cries, so they were not able to sleep, as well as the women who, seated close to his bed, and offering him every moment some surgared water, the only do-

mestic remedy which they could invent, passed
a white night.

On the following day, the door of the farm-
house was closed all morning. The wounded
man seemed to be better: the children, their eyes
reddened from lack of sleep, remained motionless in the corral, seated on the manure-heap,
following dully the motions of the animals which
were being raised there.

Teresa watched the plain through the closed
door, and entered afterward into her husband's
room. . . . How many people! All the neighbourhood was passing over the road in the direction of Pimentó's house; a swarm of men
could be seen thronging around it. And all of
them with sad and frowning faces shouting with
energetic motions, from a distance, and casting
glances of hatred toward old Barret's farm-
house.

Batiste received this news with grunts. Something itched in his breast, hurting him. The
movement of the plain toward the house of his
enemy meant that Pimentó was in a serious condition; perhaps he was dead! He was sure that
the two shots from his gun were in his body.

And now, what was going to happen? Would

he die in prison like poor Barret? No; the customs of the *huerta* would be respected; faith in justice obtained by one's own hand. The dying man would be silent, leaving it to his friends, the Terrerolas and the others, to avenge him. And Batiste did not know which to fear more, the justice of the city, or that of the *huerta*.

It was drawing toward evening, when the wounded man, despite the protests and cries of the two women, sprang out of bed.

He was stifling; his athletic body, accustomed to fatigue, was not able to stand so many hours of inactivity. The weight in his shoulder forced him to change his position, as if this would free him from pain.

With a hesitating step, benumbed by lying in bed so long, he went forth from his house and seated himself on the brick-bench beneath the vine-arbour.

The afternoon was disagreeable; the wind blew too freshly for the season; heavy dark clouds covered the sun, and the light was sinking under them, closing up the horizon like a curtain of pale gold.

Batiste looked uncertainly in the direction of the city, turning his back toward the farm-house of Pimentó, which could be seen clearly now that the fields were stripped of the golden grain which hid it before the harvest.

There might be noted in the wounded man both the impulse of curiosity and the fear of seeing too much; but at last his will was conquered, and he slowly turned his gaze toward the house of his enemy.

Yes; many people swarmed before the door; men, women, children; all the people of the plain who were anxiously running to visit their fallen liberator.

How they must hate him! . . . They were distant, but nevertheless he guessed that his name must be on the lips of all; in the buzzing of his ears, in the throbbing of his feverish temples he thought he perceived the threatening murmur of that wasp's nest.

And yet, God knew that he had done nothing more than defend himself; that he wished only to keep his own without harming any one. Why should *he* take the blame of being in conflict with these people, who, as Don Joaquín, the master, said, were very good but very stupid?

The afternoon closed in; the twilight, grey and sad, sifted over the plain. The wind, growing

continually stronger, carried toward the farm-
house the distant echo of lamentations and furious voices.

Batiste saw the people eddying in the door of
the distant farm-house, saw arms extended with
a sorrowful expression, clenched hands which
snatched handkerchief from head and cast it in
fury to the ground.

The wounded man felt all his blood mounting
toward his heart, which stopped beating for some
instants, as if paralysed, and afterward began to
thump with more fury, shooting a hot, red wave
to his face.

He guessed what was happening yonder: his
heart told him. Pimentó had just died.

Batiste felt cold and afraid, with a sensation
of weakness as if suddenly all his strength had
left him; and he went into his farm-house, not
breathing easily until he saw the door closed and
the candle lit.

The evening was dismal. Sleep overwhelmed
the family, dead tired from the vigil of the preceding night. Almost immediately after supper, they retired: before nine, all were in
bed.

Batiste felt that his wound was better. The

weight in the shoulder diminished: the fever was not so fierce; but now a strange pain in his heart was tormenting him.

In the darkness of the bedroom, still awake, he saw a pale figure rising up, at first indefinite, then little by little taking form and colour, till it became Pimentó as he had seen him the last few days, with his head bandaged and the threatening gesture of one stubbornly bent upon revenge.

The vision bothered him and he closed his eyes in order to sleep.   Absolute darkness; sleep was overpowering him, but his closed eyes were beginning to fill the dense gloom with red points which kept growing larger, forming spots of various colours; and the spots, after floating about capriciously, joined themselves together, amalgamated, and again there stood Pimentó, who approached him slowly, with the cautious ferocity of an evil beast which fascinates its victim.

Batiste tried to free himself from the nightmare.

He did not sleep; he heard his wife snoring close to him, and his sons overcome with weariness, but all the while he was hearing them

lower and lower, as if some mysterious force
were carrying the farm-house away, far away,
to a distance: and he there inert, unable to
move, no matter how hard he tried, saw the face
of Pimenó close to his own, and felt in his nostrils his enemy's hot breath.

But was he not dead? . . . His dulled brain
kept asking this question, and after many efforts,
he answered himself that Pimentó had died.
Now he did not have a broken head as before:
his body was exposed, torn by two wounds,
though Batiste was not able to determine where
they were; but two wounds he had, two inexhaustible fountains of blood, which opened livid lips.
The two gunshots, he already knew it: he was
not one to miss his aim.

And the phantom, enveloping his face with its
burning breath, fixed a glance upon him which
pierced his eyes, and descended lower and lower
until it tore his very vitals.

"Pardon, Pimentó!" groaned the wounded
man, terrified by the nightmare, and trembling
like a child.

Yes, he ought to forgive him. He had killed
him, it was true; but he should consider that he
had been the first to attack him. Come! Men

who are men ought to be reasonable! It was he who was to blame!

But the dead do not listen to reason, and the spectre, behaving like a bandit, smiled fiercely, and with a bound, landed on the bed, and seated himself upon him, pressing upon the sick man's wound with all his weight.

Batiste groaned painfully, unable to move and cast off the heavy mass. He tried to persuade him, calling him Toni with familiar tenderness, instead of designating him by his nickname.

"Toni, you are hurting me!"

That was just what the phantom wished, to hurt him, and not satisfied with this, he snatched from him with his glance alone his rags and bandages, and afterward sank his cruel nails into the deep wound, and pulled apart the edges, making him scream with pain.

"Ay! Ay! . . . Pimentó, pardon me!"

Such was his pain that his tremblings, surging up from the shoulder to his head, made his cropped hair bristle, and stand erect, and then it began to curl with the contraction of the pain until it turned into a horrible tangle of serpents.

Then a horrible thing happened. The ghost, seizing him by his strange hair, finally spoke.

"Come . . . come . . ." it said, pulling him along.

It dragged him along with superhuman swiftness, led him flying or swimming, he did not
know which, across a space both light and slippery; dizzily they seemed to float toward a red
spot which stood out in the far, far distance.

The stain grew larger, it looked in shape like
the door of his bedroom, and after it poured out
a dense, nauseating smoke, a stench of burning
straw which prevented him from breathing.

It must be the mouth of hell: Pimentó would
hurl him into it, into the immense fire whose
splendour lit up the door. Fear conquered his
paralysis. He gave a fearful cry, finally moved
his arms, and with a back stroke of his hand,
hurled Pimentó and the strange hair away from
him.

Now he had his eyes well opened; the phantom
had disappeared. He had been dreaming: it
was doubtless a feverish nightmare: now he
found himself again in bed with poor Teresa,
who, still dressed, was snoring laboriously at his
side.

But no; the delirium continued. What
strange light was illumining his bedroom? He

still saw the mouth of hell, which was like the door of his room, ejecting smoke and ruddy splendour. Was he asleep? He rubbed his eyes, moved his arms, and sat up in bed.

No: he was awake and wide awake.

The door was growing redder all the time, the smoke was denser, he heard muffled cracklings as of cane-brake bursting, licked by tongues of flame, and even saw the sparks dance, and cling like flies of fire to the cretonne curtain which closed the room. He heard a desperate steady barking, like a furiously tolling bell sounding an alarm.

Christ! . . . The conviction of reality suddenly leaped to his mind, and maddened him.

"Teresa! Teresa! . . . Up!"

And with the first push, he flung her out of bed. Then he ran to the children's room, and with shouts and blows pulled them out in their shirts, like an idiotic, frightened flock which runs before the stick without knowing where it is going. The roof of his room was already burning, casting a shower of sparks over the bed.

To Batiste, blinded by the smoke, the minutes seemed like centuries till he got the door open; and through it, maddened with terror, all the

family rushed out in their nightclothes and ran
to the road.

Here, a little more serene, they took count.

All; they were all there, even the poor dog
which howled sadly as it watched the burning
house.

Teresa embraced her daughter, who, forgetting
her danger, trembled with shame, upon seeing
herself in her chemise in the middle of the
huerta, and seated herself upon a sloping bank,
shrinking up with modesty, resting her chin upon
the knees, and drawing down her white linen
night-robe in order to cover her feet.

The two little ones, frightened, took refuge
in the arms of their elder brother, and the father
rushed about like a madman, roaring maledictions.

Thieves! How well they had known how to
do it! They had set fire to the farm-house from
all four sides, it had burst into flames from top
to bottom; even the corral with its stable and its
sheds was crowned with flames.

From it there came forth desperate neighings,
cacklings of terror, fierce gruntings; but the
farm-house, insensible to the wails of those who
were roasting in its depths, went on sending up

curved tongues of fire through the door and the windows; and from its burning roof there rose an enormous spiral of white smoke, which reflecting the fire took on a rosy transparency.

The weather had changed: the night was calm, the wind did not blow and the blue of the sky was dimmed only by the columns of smoke, between whose white wisps the curious stars appeared.

Teresa was struggling with her husband, who, recovered from his painful surprise, and spurred on by his interests, which incited him to commit follies, wished to enter the fiery inferno. Just one moment, nothing more: only the time necessary to take from the bedroom the little sack of money, the profit of the harvest.

Ah! Good Teresa! Even now it was no longer necessary to restrain the husband, who endured her violent grasp. A farm-house soon burns; straw and canes love fire. The roof came down with a crash,—that erect roof which the neighbours looked upon as an insult—and out of the enormous bed of live-coals arose a frightful column of sparks, in whose uncertain and vacillating light the *huerta* seemed to move with fantastic grimaces.

The sides of the corral stirred heavily as if

within them a legion of demons were rushing about and striking them. Engarlanded with flame the fowls leaped forth, trying to fly, though burning alive.

A piece of wall of mud and stakes fell, and through the black breach there came forth like a lightning flash, a terrible monster, ejecting smoke through its nostrils, shaking its mane of sparks, desperately beating its tail like a broom of flame, which scattered a stench of burning hair.

It was the horse. With a prodigious bound, he leaped over the family, and ran madly through the fields, instinctively seeking the canal, into which he fell with the sizzling hiss of red-hot iron when it strikes water.

Behind him, dragging itself along like a drunken demon emitting frightful grunts, came another spectre of fire, the pig, which fell to the ground in the middle of the field, burning like a torch of grease.

There remained now only the walls and the grape-vines with their twisted runners distorted by fire, and the posts, which stood up like bars of ink over the red background.

Batistet, in his longing to save something, ran

recklessly over the paths, shouting, beating at the doors of the neighbouring farm-houses, which seemed to wink in the reflection of the fire.

"Help! Help! Fire! Fire!"

His shouts died away, raising a funereal echo, like that heard amid ruins and in cemeteries.

The father smiled cruelly. He was calling in vain. The *huerta* was deaf to them. There were eyes within those white farm-houses, which looked curiously out through the cracks; perhaps there were mouths which laughed with infernal glee, but not one generous voice to say "Here I am!"

Bread! At what a cost it is earned! And how evil it makes man!

In one farm-house there was burning a pale light, yellowing and sad. Teresa, confused by her misfortune, wished to go there to implore help, with the hope of some relief, of some miracle which she longed for in their misfortune.

Her husband held her back with an expression of terror. No: not there. Anywhere but there.

And like a man who has fallen low, so low that he already is unable to feel any remorse, he shifted his gaze from the fire and fixed it on that pale light, yellowish and sad; the light of a taper